Read what the critics say about Chris McKinney

The Tattoo

"A book about the 'sins of the fathers'... A gritty, troubling book and he's done it well. The issues he raises are key to Hawaii today and for future generations."

—*The Honolulu Advertiser*

"Unforgettable...If McKinney's ultimate achievement is his portrayal of Hawaiian culture in a way that mainland Americans—those who've never seen, nor ever will, anything but the touristy side of Hawai'i—can identify with, then the ultimate failure belongs to the mainland American publishing houses for ignoring the book for so long."

—*San Antonio Current*

"Rough-and-tumble, rife with fully drawn badass characters and plenty of action, McKinney's novel is powerful and strong."

—*Time Out Chicago*

"McKinney's very first novel is thought provoking and revealing to say the least. The way this first-time novelist keeps the story moving is a credit to his skill as a writer...We highly recommend this book to those who enjoy contemporary fiction...."

—*The Dispatch*

Boi No Good

"...it's the little things, the subtle truths, that will resonate most with Hawaii readers. Things like the importance of family and passing down names, or the cultural significance of bones are the kind of details that Kahaluu-raised McKinney is undeniably talented at capturing."

—*Misty-Lynn Sanico, The Honolulu Advertiser*

"McKinney plumbs these lower depths in interior monologues that are hair-raising in their power and precision. But his story also scales the heights of Honolulu society."

—*Don Wallace, Honolulu Weekly*

"McKinney writes about contemporary Hawaii, rather than historical Hawaii, because he is 'obsessed with getting it right.'"

—*Tiffany Edwards Hunt, Big Island Chronicle*

The Queen of Tears

"McKinney vividly recreates Seoul during the Korean War from the beat-up cars made of beer cans to the affluent homes lined with fish ponds and grape vines…It's a technically skillful achievement in a story deceptively disguised as a slim, fast read."

—*Honolulu Weekly*

"McKinney's portrait of a besieged woman within a multicultural, multigenerational family saga poignantly and powerfully dramatizes the troubles women face, the pan-Asian melting pot of Hawaiian culture, and the conflicts inherent in Americanization."

—Booklist

"McKinney demonstrates a talent for restraint and tight pacing."

—*Publishers Weekly*

"Renewing and revitalizing the genre of Hawai'i noir fiction, Chris McKinney tells his tales of Honolulu's lower depth with an insider's authority and the zeal of a real writer. Beyond all that rings true in McKinney's fiction, what elevates it most is the author's unexpected compassion for those at the bottom or in emotional jeopardy."

—Tom Farber, author of *A Lover's Question*

"[An] interesting case of Korean, Korean American, and Hawaiian characters...[McKinney] has a keen eye for details of places and people. The storyline is well developed...McKinney is pitch-perfect on the social and racial climate of Hawaiians, Asians, immigrants, mixed-bloods, and whites...The frequent dialogues are crisp and pointed."

—*Korean Quarterly*

Bolohead Row

"McKinney is exceptionally skilled at imagining compelling characters, who worm their way into the consciousness of even reluctant readers... If his aim is to provoke self-righteous middle-class Islanders into awareness and understanding of the folks who populate *Bolohead Row*, he succeeds. [It] is well written and potentially very important for its ability to reflect..."

—*The Honolulu Advertiser*

"With *Bolohead Row*, McKinney officially establishes himself as the state's young breakout writer, and singlehandedly creates the genre of hardboiled Honolulu fiction."

—*Honolulu Weekly*

"What makes this book work is McKinney's "talk story" approach. He allows the reader to "sit down" and listen as Charlie tells us about his struggles. Through his journey—which includes drugs, violence and even murder—he begins to find a way to let go of the "game" and start concentrating on "life."

—*Hawaii Magazine*

Mililani Mauka

"...*Mililani Mauka* explores new emotional and physical terrain, and promises to grow the Honolulu Community College professor's audience..."

—Ragnar Carlson, *Honolulu Weekly*

"McKinney's brand of dark, underbelly portraits of contemporary Hawaii delves into lives upturned instead of buoyed by Oahu's false suburban promises."

—Christine Thomas, *Honolulu Advertiser*

"McKinney's talent in this book is to bring flawed characters to life and still allow us to make a sympathetic attachment to them."

—Stephen Hong, Asian American Literature Fan

"...In *Mililani Mauka* he [has] created a character who takes revenge in a rather spectacular but ineffectual way on a community that he feels has failed him."

—Wanda Adams, *Honolulu Advertiser*

the
red-
headed
hawaiian

Other books by Chris McKinney

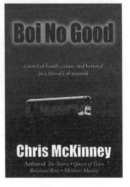

the red-headed hawaiian

Rudy Puana, M.D. and Chris McKinney

Mutual Publishing

ISBN: 978-1939487-29-2
Library of Congress Control Number: 2014932105

First Printing, April 2014

Mutual Publishing, LLC
1215 Center Street, Suite 210
Honolulu, Hawaii 96816
Ph: (808) 732-1709
Fax: (808) 734-4094
e-mail: info@mutualpublishing.com
www.mutualpublishing.com

Printed in South Korea

Dedicated to my wife Lynn for sticking with me all these crazy years and sleepless nights on call. To my family who made me who I am, especially my mom who taught me to never give up no matter what. And to my guardian angel, Simeon, who guided me back home and still reminds me of why I love Hawaii and its people.

—Rudy Puana, M.D.

Contents

Foreword

When people ask me where I'm from, and I tell them Kahaluu, the most common reaction is: "Kahaluu? Wow, you're lucky. It's so beautiful there."

I sympathize with this response. Kahaluu is a small coastal village on the east coast of Oahu. It's fronted by a barrier reef and backed by a towering, three-thousand foot green mountain range. To this day, it's relatively undeveloped—no malls, supermarkets, hotels, or factories. In fact, this photogenic coast has been captured in movies like *The Karate Kid II* and *50 First Dates.*

However, like many backwoods, rural American towns, the Kahaluu I grew up in has its share of poverty and all the baggage that comes with it. Drugs. Domestic violence. High unemployment. When I was a kid, dealers pushed at the bus stop ten feet away from my driveway. Sometimes, we'd see fifteen versus fifteen, family versus family brawls shut down late night traffic. I have one brother who went to federal prison for seven years and a cousin who spent almost all of the last two decades incarcerated by the state. Two of my siblings had kids before they hit twenty. Neither graduated from high school.

It's a place where it's not shocking to see a neighbor chase his brother down the street armed with a kitchen knife. Years later, this same neighbor ran his wife off the road, shot her, then shot himself. Growing up, I've seen hanging wild boar carcasses stripped of steaming entrails, friends who attacked a freshly cooked pot of white rice as if its the first meal they'd seen in days, and severed dog heads floating in the muddy, brackish surf. In a lot of ways, Kahaluu is like the mean head cheerleader in school—pretty on the outside, but an ugly, sawed-off bitch on the inside.

This is where my friend Rudy Puana and I were raised. To this day, the fact that he is a doctor astounds me. We grew up knowing what welfare, workman's comp, and twenty-cent bags were well before ever discovering that graduate school existed. As kids, we were taught that toughness is determined by how well we could take a punch, that violence is the most effective tool of self-empowerment, and that a life captained by unfortunate tides and currents is good enough as long as we could hang on and stay on the boat. What we learned as adults is all this is wrong.

Rudy Puana is the only doctor from Kahaluu that I know of. He's the only self-made multi-millionaire from Kahaluu that I know of. Everyone who grew up with him is, of course, proud. This story is about a red-headed Hawaiian boy who made good. Hopefully, other kids from towns like ours read it and discover that through sheer will, hard work, and a bit of luck, anything is possible.

—Chris McKinney

Blood pressure drops to seventy-four over forty-eight. Oxygen saturation plummets under eighty. Pulse races to one-eighteen. Respiratory rate elevates to thirty-five times a minute.

To a doctor, this is what death looks like. While running the critical care unit at one of the largest cancer treatment centers in the world, I'd seen it over a thousand times before.

Only this time, it was me.

The patient was a thirty-seven-year-old doctor, wife, two kids. The night before, I'd been sleeping in a hotel room and woke up at two a.m., burning up with chills. I took my temperature—104—much too high for an adult. I swallowed eight-hundred milligrams of ibuprofen and tried to go back to sleep. Several hours later, I woke up, still feverish, but I had to go to work. In medicine, there's an adage: you are never sicker than your patient. I hadn't missed a day of work in ten years.

I set off for the clinic in Kahului, Maui, one of several I've set up in places where there are rural, underserved populations—as well as the odd, off-the-grid multimillionaire and even billionaire. When I showed up at the clinic my friend Frank, also a doctor, and his wife Malia, a nurse, diagnosed me: I looked like crap. Malia took my temperature—still 104. They gave me more ibuprofen, a hundred milligrams of Tylenol, and sixty milligrams of Toradol. I told them I just needed to lay down for a bit. We had patients to see that day. Instead, they put me on a plane and sent me back home, to Kona.

The Toradol kicked in on the thirty-minute plane ride from Maui to the Big Island, and I was feeling a bit better. It was probably just a bad flu. I felt bad for leaving Frank with all those patients, so I decided I'd buy him a pitching wedge on my way home to make up for it. Yeah, I know. Doctors and golf. Doctors and sleep is another one. I'd desperately tried to get some sleep during the flight.

By the time I landed, the drugs were wearing off. I shivered and sweated as I staggered through the airport. Light-headed and exhausted, I headed to the parking lot. I slumped in my car, then rallied and drove to Sports Authority to pick up Frank's golf club. After buying the wedge, I headed home. Dizziness hit and I had trouble breathing. I swerved off the road and called my wife. She wanted to come and pick me up. But in stubborn man-fashion, I told her I could make it. The car lurched home, and I wondered why I'd made the call in the first place. Maybe I just wanted someone to worry and cheer me on.

When I got home, my wife Lynn took one look at me and knew I was really sick. I couldn't argue with her: we'd met in med school and she was a doctor as well. However, she also knew how stubborn I was, so she called for a second opinion— our friend, Ron Ah Loy. Ron was triple-certified in internal medicine, gastroenterology, and infectious diseases. He was one of the best doctors Lynn and I had ever met, and we'd met hundreds over the years.

Ron was a Big Island boy and Native Hawaiian like me. He came right over, looked at me for about three seconds and said, "Either I'm calling an ambulance or I'm driving you to the E.R. myself."

That's when I got worried.

At the hospital, Ron stuck an I.V. in me, gave me antibiotics, put me on oxygen, and ordered a chest x-ray.

My right lung was full of fluid.

My left was about a quarter full.

This is when I saw the numbers: blood pressure, o2 sat, respiratory rate, pulse. I thought of the hundreds of patients I'd seen who'd registered similar numbers. I remembered Patrick, twenty-five-years-old, who'd talked till the end. We had been chatting about Longhorn football when he looked at me as if I'd tapped him on the shoulder. He'd smiled, politely thanked me, then died. With Patrick, I'd wanted to crawl in a corner and never come to work again.

I remembered Simeon. The massive Hawaiian with the massive family and unfortunately, a massive case of cancer as well. I was at a craps table at a Vegas casino when he'd passed. (I know: doctors and Vegas. But I was living in Texas then, and he'd wanted to die at home, in the Islands.) After I got the call, I went up to my room and cried.

Now I was dying like Patrick. I was dying like Simeon. I was dying like the hundreds of others. Ron told me I had strep pneumo, a rare strain of pneumonia. I knew that it was the same strain that killed celebrities Jim Henson and Bernie Mac. By this time, I was coughing up pink froth out of my mouth. I was breathing so hard, I couldn't talk. Try talking after sprinting a quarter-mile full-blast. That's what it felt like. I communicated by writing frantic notes with a Sharpie.

Ron put me on Levophed, a last-ditch medication to bring up my blood pressure. We doctors had a nickname for Levophed: Leave-um-dead.

Woozy, I calculated my Apache score—liver enzymes, arterial blood saturation, heart rate. I wished I wasn't a doctor. I wished I didn't *know* what was going on. I had a less than one percent chance of surviving.

During the next twenty-four hours, I slipped in and out of consciousness. I was now a patient in the critical care unit I ran. Even though I was delusional and more scared than I'd ever been in my life, when I'd snap awake, I'd write orders, and unfortunately, people listened.

Worse, while I knew the protocol I did everything I could to avoid it. First, I needed a breathing tube, but breathing tubes to me meant death, so I scribbled orders to the staff to *not* insert one. Instead I convinced them to stick me on a tubeless ventilator strapped to my face, called bipap. Sleep was good, too, because my breathing rate decreased while I slept, but I told the nurses to wake me up if my o2 levels dropped below eighty-five, because o2 levels below eighty-five in my experience also meant death. So the nurses woke me up when my oxygen levels dropped, and I wrote orders while gasping for air and coughing up blood. Not surprising that I hardly slept. But even more stupid.

When I knew there was no getting out of having a catheter stuck in my heart, I refused to let just anyone do it. I'd seen some of these people try to stick septic patients before. They sucked at it. I was the one the hospital called to stick people. I told Lynn to call Frank. He was the only one I trusted. Frank, who looked more like a tattoo-covered white supremacist biker than a doctor, walked in wearing shorts, slippers, and a tank top. He plunged the giant needle in me. Thankfully, he did not miss; he never missed. Insisting on Frank was my one bit of stubbornness that paid off.

So there I was, loopy, frightened, and barely conscious. Between hallucinating little men playing basketball on my chest and dead people walking in and out of my hospital room, I was telling the doctors and nurses what to do. Overseeing my own treatment.

I don't remember a lot of this, and this story is partially pieced together by what my wife had told me later. But I do remember that my favorite nurses avoided me because they didn't want to jinx me. I remember that my parents and sisters flew into town to be with me. I remember dreaming about a friend, a girl who I had not seen in twenty years. In my dream, she drove me to her house and showed me around. White pillars on the outside. Cozy, pillowed orange sectional sofas on the inside. She kept telling me she was taking me to the farm. What farm, I had no idea.

I also remember holding my son, thinking it'd be the last time. I cried and cried for the first time in years. *This is not happening*, I thought.

But most of all, I remember after breathing hard for two days straight, staying awake got harder and harder. Time became more difficult to keep track of. Scribbling notes took monumental effort. I was exhausted and with that the terror faded.

Finally, I was ready to die.

2.

When you have no future, you spend a lot of time thinking about the past. Kids teasing me by singing Rudy the Red-headed Human during the holidays. My dad's forty-eight-foot sampan blasting past the head buoy outside Kaneohe Bay. Fishing for mahi-mahi. The iridescent bright blues and greens of the mahi-mahi gradually turning yellow as the fish tired and was ready to surrender to death. Nebraska winters. Sheets of snow clinging to a-framed barns and churches. The sight of Texas from a twin-engine airplane. Vast tracts of never-ending dry land sectioned off in squares. I thought about my mother, full of love and bad cooking. I remembered Lynn dressed as a Spice Girl at a Halloween party, the night we first started dating. They were very much alike, my wife and mother. My kids, Sam and my baby daughter Gigi, would be fine without me.

I was too tired to have regrets. Besides, I'd lived a pretty good life. I was a Kahaluu oddity—a red-headed Hawaiian boy. That's right, a Hawaiian with red hair. Descended from fishermen, plumbers, and brawlers, a boy who made good:

"Heard Rudy one doctor?"

"Rudy? Fricking guy barely grad high school. No way."

"Yup, sucka must make big bucks now."

"Rudy? The red-headed Hawaiian boy? The one used to steal boats and play basketball naked? No way, the buggah was always funny, but not too smart."

"Yup. Must be the parents, ah?"

In Kahaluu, the small town on the eastside of Oahu where I grew up, there were haole things, like dress shoes, studying in school, and talking for a living. Then there were Hawaiian things, like nature, thick-skinned bare feet, and earning a living with hard hands. Kahaluu did not produce associate medical directors at world-renowned cancer treatment centers. It bred construction workers, small-boat fishermen and pig farmers, but also welfare queens, drug addicts, and petty criminals.

People like my father. Three-hundred pounds of scars and ink casually piloting a boat in the midst of twenty foot swells. It bred the likes of my grandfather, a full-blooded Hawaiian, as well. Racing his dumptruck down Maunalani Heights, a whirl of dust, soot, and asbestos kicking up from the floorboard and working its way up, Grandpa not even squinting as the particles swirled throughout the cab. When you're Native Hawaiian, and ninety percent of your people get wiped off the face of the earth in a little over a hundred years, you have to be tough to endure.

But by day two in critical care, I didn't want to endure. Remembering was all I had strength for and that was good enough.

Later, my wife told me they put me on Xigris, yet another experimental drug known as a last-ditch measure. When I slipped into sleep, nobody knew if I'd be waking up.

Chapter One

Hanau (Born)

Sometimes I wonder what it must've been like when my big, black monster of a Hawaiian father saw me for the first time. No way his keiki could be that squalling redhead. And not strawberry red or blondish red. Red. Bozo the Clown kine. My friends used to tell me I looked like a walking match. Men like my Dad don't faint, but a part of me likes to imagine him taking one look and swooning.

Dad had broad shoulders and massive cranial features. He was over half-Hawaiian. He was covered with tattoos before ink was in style, and his knuckles were scarred and disfigured from years of brawling, fishing, and getting into drunken fights with walls. Unlike most people who could point to the few scars on their body, tell stories with a grin, and sprinkle the word "kolohe" here and there, Dad never spoke about his trophies. Maybe it was because he had so many it would be like asking a fry cook to describe every burger he ever flipped. Dad was that hardcore local heavy you may have known who pushed around less intimidating guys, and especially red-headed haoles, for no reason. Ironic. But also, as I grew older, confusing—I was his son but I looked like his favorite punching bag.

On the other hand, Mom was a fair-skinned, dirty blonde. She had both Caucasian and Hawaiian blood (about a third), but the haole dominated her features. At least it couldn't have been a complete shock when they saw their pale-skinned, red-headed newborn.

Before me, my mother and father had three daughters and were impatiently awaiting someone who could pass on the family name. In fact, they were also anxious to pass on my father's first name. By the way, Dad's name is Rudolph Puana. Rudolph.

You would figure that when my parents saw a small, skinny white boy with red hair come out of my mom, my only Hawaiian features an upepe nose and the bossing frontal forehead, they would've thought—"uh-oh, reindeer games!"—and held off on the reindeer name. But of course, they didn't. As I grew into a little kid, the holidays became nightmarish. My friends and relatives called me opakapaka, Christmas tree, and sang the number one hit of the sound track of my life: Rudolph the Red-headed Human.

Even during the eleven months that weren't Christmas, my life was a trial, kind of like Johnny Cash's "A Boy Named Sue" (the number two hit in the sound track of my life). In that song, "Sue's" father finally explains that he gave him the name so he'd grow up to be a man, "with gravel in his guts and spit in his eye," ready to fight at the slightest sneer. Only I hated to fight. Which was truly a sad state of affairs because on my side of the island of Oahu, in Kahaluu, fighting was a forgone conclusion if you were a guy whose name was Sue—or, if you looked liked me, Rudolph.

So there I was, a Hawaiian boy who didn't look the part. I was that crazy rabbit on *America's Funniest Home Videos*, the one that was raised with a house full of dogs and thought it was one. It would bark, gnaw on soup bones, and even go through the doggie door to poop outside. That was me growing up—the crazy barking rabbit.

"Don't act like that!"

"Kuli kuli kanak!"

"Hey haole boy like beef?"

I was quite confused in my early days.

Like most children I looked to my parents for guidance, but their advice was often contradictory. My father only embraced The Hawaiian Way, while my mother, perhaps in reaction, subscribed to The Haole Way. Even though she was part Hawaiian, when it came to her kids, my mom forbade pidgin in the house. Dad spoke nothing but da kine pidgin—but only outside of the house (God forbid he break mom's rules). My mother stressed the importance of doing well academically whereas my dad, who labored with his hands and fished for extra cash on weekends, taught me the value of physical labor like his father had before him.

Grandpa, like everyone else in our family, was a hard worker, but he was also a hard drinker. Occasionally, he would ride his horse straight into the neighborhood bar and order a drink. Being a boxing prodigy in Maui at a very young age, Grandpa was someone you didn't mess with. Everyone knew the routine. Grandpa would put the horse away, get drunk and try to pick a fight, sometimes not in that order.

Unfortunately for my dad, the fun didn't stop at the bar, and my grandfather would come home drunk and frequently beat his sons along with the horse. My father had to quickly learn how not to piss off the old man.

When Dad was twelve, Grandpa pulled him and his older brother out of school so they could build an addition to the Maunalani house to make room for a rapidly growing family. They got walking orders from Grandpa at dawn and worked until his return at night. During the day, my father and his brother hauled lumber up the steep hills of Maunalani Heights. Then they carefully sawed supports and stacked wood under the house. They jacked it straight up in the air, inch-by-inch. This went on, day after day, until the house was ten feet higher and a second story could be built under the single-wall constructed dwelling. Let me reiterate—Dad was twelve-years-old. Turning a one-story house into a two-story one was his sixth grade curriculum.

When my father wasn't busy being smacked around by his drunk father or being pulled out of school to perform hard labor, he became proficient in two things: fighting and spear fishing.

I'd once heard that when women imagine their mothers as young ladies, they envision them dancing. I'm guessing that when local boys imagine their fathers' childhoods, they picture them shirtless, ripped, and young, bobbing from side-to-side, popping jabs and growling profanities. Beefing, we called it. But not me. Though I have often imagined my father fighting, I've always preferred to picture him diving. I still see Dad helping Grandpa load his work truck with pipes and tools in the dark before his morning trip to the beach. I see him as he grabs a bite from Grandma who's busy preparing breakfast, lunch, and dinner for a husband and ten kids before she goes to work at the rectory at Star of the Sea school.

After a quick bite and loading the truck, Dad jumps into Grandpa's old work truck, ready for the day ahead. The truck is crammed with plumbing supplies, crud, and empty homebrew jars (Grandpa loved his okolehao), and rattles while it races down the dirt road to the shore. Finally Grandpa brakes in front of the beach and lets the killer out.

Dad's dark and skinny, so dark some of his friends call him purple. Barefoot and shirtless, he strolls to the side of the truck in the cold, early morning, reaches over the truck's sidewall, and grabs his gear. As far as gear goes, nothing special. A short three-prong spear, a homemade mask, fins, and a huge inner-tube. Inside this large, floating donut, rigged netting recycled from an old lay-net. The net is fastened inside with double-layered mesh and is attached to the inner tube with lashings made of multi-colored scraps of rope. The tube itself is almost bursting with air because by the end of the day, the net will be stretched to its limits, the tube practically sinking from all the fish. For Dad the hardest part of the day will be getting the inner tube out of the water after the massacre. But he doesn't complain. First, because no one complains to my grandfather, and second, he will do anything to impress his dad.

Dad sits at the shore with a pile of gear that resembles a heap of trash. His gear, plastered with old scales and dried blood, reeks like low tide. With hardly a word between the two, Pops drives away.

After Pops leaves, Dad drags his gear near the water's edge. He wets his feet so that he can slip his fins on. After putting on his fins and stepping in the water, he spits a large wad of saliva into his mask and swirls it around to keep the glass from fogging up. He prefers rubbing naupaka leaves in his mask, but he forgot to grab some before he arrived at the shore. It's Oahu before the naupaka in the area will be annihilated to make room for yet-another construction project.

Dad puts on the old, leaky mask, drags his tube in the water, and throws his spear into the deep. He makes the sign of the cross and jumps in. The next person who will see him, besides the occasional fisherman, is Grandpa picking him up after work at five PM.

As Dad hunts the coastline, he's not thinking one fish at a time. Before he spears his fourth catch, he's already eyeing the turtle off to the side. He hits the red uhu, quickly tosses it the inner tube, then stalks the turtle. He slings his spear and lets go.

He struggles as he pulls the now-dead turtle up to the surface and flips it upside down in the inner tube. Sharks are now following. But he knows every shark from Ala Moana to Kewalo Basin by name, and they all know him as well. Nobody takes anything from my dad without a fight, and the sharks apparently know it.

At the end of the day, it takes both my father and grandfather to drag the inner tube, reeking of blood and fish gut, out of the water.

2.

After years and years of diving and growing into a hard-hitting, hard-drinking adult, my father found better and better ways to make his living in the water. Some ideas were smarter than others, but they all made money. By the time he was in his early twenties, married, and starting his own family, he was diving for black coral, which could only be found in depths below 150 feet. With a dinged-up fire extinguisher converted to a dive tank that looked more suitable for welding than scuba strapped to his back, Dad swam down to the bottom of deep blue channels. There was no pressure gauge attached to his tank, no fancy dive watch fastened around his wrist. He knew it was time to stop when the air started running out.

The money was great; in fact, for my father, who at this point had two daughters to support (my sister Kathy and I were not born yet), it was more lucrative than taking plumbing jobs with Grandpa. However, the risk for a young father was high. Dad lost good friends to black coral diving. It almost took him as well.

At twenty-eight, Dad stopped diving for good after his second trip to the decompression chamber. Once again, from below two-hundred feet, he was running out of oxygen and swam too quickly to the surface. During his ascent, he bruised a nerve in his spine.

At the hospital, fighting off paralysis while pissing into a plastic bag, he swore to God he'd never dive again if He got him out of this one. Having the bends was excruciating, but of course it was the thought of being crippled and having zero bowel control for the rest of his life that scared him more than anything else. Sure enough, God pulled through. My father would do all his fishing from aboard a boat after that.

3.

Obviously the ocean was always my dad's domain, and it's from him that I got my love for the sea. Growing up in my house as the only son, no way I could make it past fourteen without knowing how to squid, throw net, and flat-out fish. My mom used to say if the world went to crap, at least I could find food. Being the youngest, I only knew my dad as a fisherman since his diving days had been long over. He would appear on *Let's Go Fishing* with Hari Kojima. He would be in the *Hawaii Fishing News* on a regular basis, pictured with thousand-pound marlins or his usual haul of ahi during season. He and I were permanent fixtures at Heeia Kea pier where fishermen would eat and hang out. I would try my luck at catching shoreline critters. And of course, I would get teased because of my red hair.

"Fireball!"

"Richie Cunningham!"

Once, my mom bought shoes a bit too big me.

"Ronald McDonald!"

When the teasing children's parents would catch their kids picking on me then give them lickings for it, of course, it only got worse.

"Tampon head..."

I didn't even know what a tampon was back then.

Eventually the sun would set, and I would retreat to my father as he finished his card games and cases of beer. I would sit at the table and listen to the old-timers, who, unlike their kids, never teased me. They'd talk about my crazy father diving for black coral. They would talk about his partners, Perry and Adams, and how once they'd gotten bent, and as soon as the paralysis wore off, they were out of the decompression chamber and back in the water. Here was a group of the greatest Windward-side fisherman Hawaii had ever seen, racking up record after record fish, and all they talked about was how they all used to dive. To them, diving was the more masculine way to make money.

Everyone was "uncle" and "aunty" at the pier, and they all enjoyed slipping me beers under the table and watching the little red head get flushed from the alcohol. All this took place under an old rickety roof tucked away under swamp brush. Everyone called it *Da Shack*.

Da Shack was a gathering point for local fisherman on our side of the island. Both professional fisherman and weekend warriors got together, talked story, played illegal poker games, and of course drank the entire time.

Admittedly, *Da Shack* was a dump. This place would have been condemned the day after being built if someone had submitted a permit application. Rectangular in shape, it was made up of layers of old plywood and mismatched paneling. It contained an old "donated" sink straight from Pearl Harbor and a large make-shift picnic bench that sat around thirty, its legs and top assembled out of pieces most likely taken from several state parks. The entire place, nestled in the middle of a swampy thatch of trees, reeked of stale beer, dried fish, and stagnant, brackish water.

People carved their names on the old, wooden bench, some I knew well. "Acey Boy," "K-bay Crew," "Pua Titas"—the usual suspects. Every last inch of *Da Shack* was built from fragments of stolen state or federal property. The electricity was "borrowed" from the utility pole near by, and the plumbing, which my father helped rig, ran from the city water line a mere fifty yards away. Everyone pitched in to make this place a home away from home, and if that meant borrowing some stuff, so be it.

Across from *Da Shack* stood a conglomeration of make-shift shanties and lean-tos that I used to call The Village. One day, on our way home from the pier, we passed The Village, and my father pointed to it and said, "That is where we used to live and raise pigs with Grandpa."

He said it in a proud voice. Through his hard work, he'd gotten us out of that hole. He was right. He did. In our house, the words "no can" were never uttered. I thought about the lumber he'd muled up Maunalani Heights as a child, the house he'd raised when he was twelve, and how he dove to life-threatening depths, not for recreation, but to make money. Most of his stories imparted the value of hard work. But when he talked about The Village, I sensed something more. He missed it.

He went on to talk about living there after he and my mother had gotten married, and how she almost shot him once when he got home from a bender. "Hell, sometimes I was gone so long she probably didn't recognize me," he said. "Yeah, that was some times."

Unfortunately, *Da Shack* and The Village were demolished when I was about ten-years-old to make way for a marina and golf course that were never built. Over one hundred Hawaiians suddenly found themselves homeless. The destruction of *Da Shack* also killed the pier community.

My father didn't have much to say about it. That was him, though. He was never talkative, and he took as much care in avoiding conversation on life's disappointments as he did concealing the hellish abuse he'd endured as a child (years later, it was Mom who told me). He hardly ever talked about his checkered, young-adult past as well. In fact, the time during his young adulthood is the most murky for me. From the bits and pieces that slipped over the years, I also learned that back then he'd taken up strong-arming for the men who controlled the underbelly of Hawaii while setting up his own illegal crap games in town. The latter paid the best because he was the stickman, the muscle, and the bookie. Apparently, the name Rudy Puana rang out in Downtown back then.

However, all that illegal stuff stopped, or so he said, when a small haole-looking Hawaiian girl from Kaimuki came into his life and refused to leave.

4.

My mother, Lealani Schwartz, was born in Honolulu and lived in places like California, Arizona, Texas, and Maui by the time she was eleven-years-old. Her father, a Romanian Jew who loved to travel and could speak eight languages, finally settled the small family on Oahu, in the Kaimuki district of Honolulu, a place that still has a small-town feel. There he opened a pharmacy. My mother, an only child, was raised in what she calls "a cultured and progressive household." Her mother was an artist who worked with porcelain, oil paints, and also designed clothes, so Mom was introduced to arts at a very early age. Grandma could take one look at a painting or dress and replicate it.

Grandma and Grandpa sent my mother to stay with her Maui grandfather so that their daughter would be schooled in Hawaiian culture. In Maui, Mom learned to pick opihi and wana, cook Hawaiian dishes like squid luau, and began her studies in the art of hula, which included how to fashion leis and skirts. But after awhile she missed her parents, so she moved back.

Things my mother heard from her parents growing up:

"You need to find your own path."

"Surround yourself with people who are smarter and more experienced than you. You will get a free education."

"Lead with your heart."

"What did you learn from that experience?"

"There is no such thing as 'cannot.'"

"We're just here to help you."

Add to this her own credit card at fourteen, and with it the freedom to fly to a neighbor island on a whim to watch a high school football game, and you can see how her only-child, middle-class, anything-goes upbringing was the opposite of my father's house-raising, fist-dodging, family of ten-feeding childhood. She didn't have chores and was never told, "You cannot do this because I said so." The only time she'd gotten hit was when she was in the sixth grade and began experimenting with four-letter words. It wasn't a hit really—just a mild slap across the head. Afterwards, Grandpa apologized profusely and bought her a pink phone.

Even though my mom had both Hawaiian and Tahitian blood, looks-wise, she pulled haole more than anything else. But she learned to fit in. She and my father met when she was fourteen and they became friends. They started dating when she was sixteen. She looked past (or directly at?) the drinking, fighting, drugs, and abusive family life and thought: I can change him.

But her father wasn't happy with what he saw as my mom's attempt at genetic variation, and the first conversation between Dad and Grandpa Schwartz had ended with Grandpa yelling, "Get the hell out of here! My daughter isn't going to be with a *nigger* like you." Grandpa, remember, was from Romania; he didn't have his racial epithets down, exactly. If he'd stopped to think, he might've remembered that "schwartz" means "black"—and not always in a complimentary way when describing a Jew, which, of course, he was.

My father invited my grandfather out to the lawn to discuss his remarks. Of course my grandpa declined. As alluded to above, he was a very smart man. However, like any parent, his intelligence was sometimes compromised by love for his child, and his next lapse in judgment came when he offered my father a brand new '57 Thunderbird to stay away from my mother. But the more you pound squid, the better it tastes. My father loved her even more after that.

The funny thing was, through all this drama, Dad was never offended that Grandpa Schwartz wanted him to stay away from my mother. If he'd had a daughter, he later said, he would have wanted her to stay clear of the likes of Rudy Puana as well.

So how did an uneducated Hawaiian with only his hands for resources and a life of gutting fish in his future get back at the highly sophisticated, multi-lingual pharmacist who had branded him with the ultimate of racial slurs? Easy, Dad knocked the educated man's daughter up, married her, and took her to live in The Village a few months later.

...............5.

When my mother married my father, she was seventeen-years-old, six months' pregnant, and found herself living in The Village on Pop's pig farm. My father gave her a gun and told her that if he wasn't home, shoot anyone who approached. The daughter of a highly-educated Jewish pharmacist, an opera fan, knocked up, and living in a quonset hut—the image still cracks me up.

But there she was. And she loved it. There were pigs, horses, cows, and chickens living with her in all that muck. She loved animals. She tamed a wild mountain dog and named him Beatnik.

Once she and my father said their "I do's," her pharmacist father's opinion of Dad spun one-eighty. In fact, my father and my mother's father had grown so close that when Grandpa passed away years later, Dad cried like a baby.

So for Mom, during those initial days of marriage, things were good. At least for the first two months. But then something shifted in my father, and he'd start disappearing at night and sometimes did not come home until the next morning. Arguments and screaming matches followed. As my mom says till this day, "He was a real son-of-a-bitch back then."

My father's rebuttal: "Work hard, play hard."

Back then, my mom accused him of choosing his friends over his family. Once, when they were having a particularly heated disagreement, my mother stuck a finger in the middle of the big man's chest and said, "You touch my kids, I'll bury you."

And she meant it.

And he never did touch us. Much. Despite all the beatings he ate as a child, he never raised a hand full of bad intentions to his wife or children. For Mom, physical abuse was a deal-breaker. She would have walked if it had ever happened. Oh, there was verbal abuse between my parents for sure, but my mother gave as good as she got. Whenever the fights would threaten to bubble into something else though, my father would drop his clenched fists and leave the house.

He'd drink with his friends and screw around with other women. Most of my mother's friends encouraged her to get a divorce. In fact, she had an attorney on retainer. Forever her father's daughter, Mom began to look at her marriage as a business. She drew out a list of assets and liabilities.

Liability: If she filed for divorce, she'd have to go on welfare.

Assets: Home (which for my mother was a sacred place), family, and no one telling her what to do.

In fact, even though Dad made the money, he turned all of his paychecks over to her without having to be asked, and she was the one who gave him an allowance. Also, she never doubted his love for their children. He'd often say, "Make sure the kids have this," then make it so by working as much over-time as it took to get it.

But he was also the same guy who, once, when he'd been in the Coast Guard, decided to drink compass liquid with his buddies. He'd told them that if they soaked the alcohol with bread, it would be safe to drink. So they drank it. My father ended up fine, but one of his friends went blind.

So my mother's list of assets outweighed her list of liabilities. She stayed and raised the kids. She let him have his fun on one condition: he had to buy a ton of life insurance.

6.

There's two versions of my mother as a parent. The first version is of a teen mom who raised two daughters under the shadow of her mother-in-law and sisters-in law. The second version is a woman who was a confident, battle-scarred, seasoned parent who decided she wanted to raise her two youngest children the way she had been raised.

My two oldest sisters, Rualani (a combination of "Rudy" and "Lealani"—definitely a child named by teenage parents) and Joann (who I used to call "The Tita") were raised by the first version of Mom. This first version was unsure of herself and therefore much more conservative. There were rules, there were punishments, there were chores, and there was some "you cannot do this because I said so." It was how Mom's sister-in-law was raising her kids, and my mother lacked maternal confidence because of her age; also, a part of her wanted to just fit in with my father's family. Like many an older child, Rualani grew to be the responsible one. She was, in fact, like a second mother to me. She'd clean my room and bought my first bike.

Joann was more like a youngest child than middle in a lot of ways. She was a terrific athlete and sometimes acted out to get attention. She'd get into fights, get drunk, and sometimes run away. There was a lot of my dad in her. She was also my protector when I was a little kid. Once, when I was getting teased by a boy much older than me at a family party (shockingly, he was ridiculing my white skin and red hair), Joann walked right up to him and lit him up. When his father found out someone named Jo had beat up his son, he came by the house to talk to my dad about it. Dad called Joann out of the house. The boy's father took one look at my sister (she was wearing a red and white muumuu), slapped his son on the back of the head, and drove away. The boy had apparently left out the fact that his bully was a girl.

There's a ten-year gap in age between Joann and the youngest of my sisters, Kathy. So Kathy and I were raised by version two of my mother. We didn't have household chores. And we were not told (by my mother at least) "You can't do that because I say so." We wanted for nothing, and there was very little in the way of rules. Like her father used to tell her, we were encouraged to "find our path."

This was not as easy as it seems for my mother. I was born a sickly child with a blood disorder (low platelets, high white blood cell count) that today would be classified as a rare type of leukemia. There were times when I'd be hospitalized for weeks at a time getting dosed with steroids. When I was six, I once urinated pure blood. Without blinking, my mother told me I drank too much fruit punch and took me, once again, to the hospital. My health got so bad that my mother moved our family from the suburbs of Enchanted Lakes, where we'd moved when they tore down The Village and did away with the pig farm, to Kahaluu. Our Enchanted Lakes house was next to a shopping center, and the doctor had told her that the fumes from the complex were making me worse.

But despite my health problems, my mother encouraged me to do whatever I wanted. Want to climb the mountain out back? Go climb it. Want to build a tree house? Go build it. I took all of my dad's old wood and built one with walls, windows, a roof, and carpet. I was twelve—a far cry from jacking up a house ten feet in the air—but I was proud of it. My best friend Binky and I constantly played in that thing.

Want to play sports? Go for it. I'll take you. Just tell me what you need. As for childhood conversations on eventual career choice? I once told my mom I wanted to be a garbage man. "Just do your best and get all the trash in the truck," she said. The only non-negotiable thing was church. My mother volunteered at St. Ann's, and I had to be an altar boy.

Of course, at the time, I didn't realize how much strength this letting go took, but now, as a parent who lives in a society inundated with warnings about the dangers our children face every day out there in the big, bad world, I cannot help but idolize her courage. All of us are lucky that we were raised by this woman, but Kathy and I were especially fortunate to get version two. My two oldest sisters both got married young, had kids, and lived lives filled with personal and financial struggles. On the other hand, Kathy went to law school, became a state prosecutor, owned a law firm, became head of the Office of Environmental Quality Control, and served as an advisor to the Governor of the State of Hawaii—all before she turned forty. As for me, I went to med school, double-boarded in anesthesiology and critical care, and became one of the youngest associate medical directors in cancer center MD Anderson's history. Our older sisters eventually became small business owners on the Mainland and came out fine, but it's hard not to wonder how they would've turned out if they'd had access to the opportunities, and go-for-it attitude, that Kathy and I had.

At other times, however, I wonder if the differences between me and Kathy and our older sisters stems from our looks. I know how that sounds. But remember Grandpa Schwartz and what he called my father? Well, Kathy and I look white while Rualani and Joann have dark hair and skin. After all, we all grew up in the same neighborhood and were raised by the same parents, and it's not like Kathy and I are any smarter—high school busted all four of our asses. So it must be prejudice, right?

Maybe. But maybe part of it is because Kathy and I got the benefit of being raised by a more confident, enlightened mother—Mom 2.0.

....

When I woke up, I didn't know how long I was at the hospital. Two days? Maybe even four? I tried to focus, but all I could make out were floating heads cutting across my line-of-sight like loose helium balloons. I knew they were people, but I could not see their torsos, and it made me think of pictures my son had drawn, pictures held up on the refrigerator with magnets, bodiless sketches of Mom, Dad, Sam, and baby Gigi, all with stick arms and legs protruding from their round, dot-eyed faces.

Two still heads floated on opposite sides of the room. They were my wife and father. They weren't speaking. I vaguely recalled something about a leaking pipe at our house and my father's refusal to leave the hospital and fix it. I wondered if my father ever drew as a kid. Probably not. He probably didn't even know what a crayon was until his first day of kindergarten. No childhood pictures on his refrigerator growing up.

Two other heads drifted in through the doorway. My sisters Rualani and Kathy. Rualani, my second mom, who cut my steak when I was a kid. Kathy, the lawyer, who would not only do anything for me, but had helped a number of my Kahaluu friends with legal trouble as well. She once received a couple of gallon Zip-loc bags stuffed with kalua pig in thanks for services rendered.

As always, it was my mom's head that hovered closest. She had that look on her face, like I was six, and she wanted to tell me I drank too much fruit punch again. I felt bad for her. This wasn't the first time she had to watch a loved one die. She was the one who took care of her father when he'd passed. And there was my Aunty Olive, my mom's best friend, who'd been forced into a wheelchair since childhood and could barely talk. Every day, my mom drove an-hour-and-a-half to the nursing home and cared for her. This had gone on for over twenty years. Mom had seen enough of death and I didn't want her here. But there she was. They were all here. Those who loved me most. Lynn eating fear and multi-tasking like mad—overseeing my treatment, my daughter Gigi (who was too young to be at the hospital), and my son, Sam, while feuding with my father over home plumbing on top of all that. My father, brooding off to the side as usual. A man so over-the-top proud of his son and daughter-in-law that once when a wedding invitation had arrived at their house and was addressed to "Dr. and Mrs. Rudy Puana," he scratched it out and wrote "THE DOCTORS PUANA" and mailed it back.

When Lynn saw that I was awake, she approached. She told me that I wasn't getting worse in that sort of half-full sort of way. I tried to talk but couldn't. I wanted to tell her about something on the news I'd seen just the week before. Something about a woman who ran away to Mexico after the death of a loved one. I was thinking how nice it would be to be able to do that. But you can't go anywhere when it's you that's dying.

You'd think I'd be grateful to have them all around me, but I wanted to tell Lynn, to tell all of them, to go away.

It was funny in a sick sort of way. I'd finally come home after spending twelve years in the Mainland busting my ass: med school—reading words like iatrogenic methemoglobinemia until my eyes burned. Residency—getting yelled at by doctors and senior residents while working the tail-end of a thirty-six hour shift. Practicing medicine—practically living at MD Anderson, the cancer center, watching hundreds of people die while hardly ever seeing my wife and kids.

Back in the Mainland, I'd had enough. I'd wanted to come home.

So I accepted a seventy-five percent pay cut and moved my family to Hawaii.

And here I was, finally home, finally back in Hawaii, and now I was dying. I wouldn't even get to live here very long.

I wondered how my dad and Pops, the toughest men I ever knew, would've handled this situation. Both would probably fight. But fighting was never my thing. Maybe the childhood leukemia took it out of me. Maybe it was in my genes, since my five-year-old son, Sam, had my smiling nature and none of his grandfather's.

At least I did have one thing over Dad, one thing Dad didn't have to put up with as a kid. Sure, he ate spectacular beatings served by his father. Yes, as a tween, he jacked up a house ten feet in the air. He decimated the marine population at Ala Moana. His life was way, way harder, no doubt. However, at least he didn't have red hair.

Chapter Two

Wa Kamalii (Childhood)

.... 1.

Growing up in Kahaluu, one of my first memories was of my mom dropping me off at school early one morning. I was getting out of the car and about to walk to a group of boys who I hardly knew when I turned to my mom and said, "Mom, why did you born me with red hair?"

She looked like I'd just hit her in the gut. She didn't say anything, so I got out of the car and headed for the group of boys who were sure to tease me.

That was my life as a little white kid. Even though I had Native blood and the last name Puana, no one looked past the red hair. It's a miracle I didn't grow up to become a clock tower sniper or a serial killer with human heads stored in my freezer. Kids are brutal. If they spot a booger in your nose on Monday, you are "Booger Boy" for the rest of your life. For me that "Monday" was the first day of school every year.

The end of summer break was always a depressing time for me growing up. While most kids dreaded going back to school because of homework, I hated it because the nine-month teasing marathon was about to begin. Kathy's birthday was at the end of summer, so we usually had a party right before school started. She and her friends would be smiling and laughing, carrying on like the next day wasn't the first day of school, so I usually ruined the festivities with a random act of idiocy to shut everyone up. I would sneeze on her birthday cake or fake a leg injury. I loved her and we got along splendidly, but I wanted someone else to feel a sliver of the pain I was about to endure the next day.

For me the first day of school was a ball of energy that built and built throughout the morning until that instant when all the forces of nature came together and exploded in one moment:

Roll call.

Kids sat in their chairs chatting with their friends. Everyone had dark summer tans. I, on the other hand, just had tanned freckles, and my hair turned a brighter red from the sun. All of the students laughed and talked about their summer vacation adventures before the teacher finally settled down the class. At this point, it hit me that the unavoidable was about to happen. It was a slow painful process because my last name started with a "P." I hoped that everyone wasn't paying attention by the time the teacher got to my name, or that this year it would be different and she would read the name "Rudy." But like clockwork:

"Rudolph?"

It didn't matter if they'd known me for years or not at all. New student or old, they all turned, spotted the red hair, and laughed. They launched into a chorus of "Rudolph the Red-Headed Human." I'd try to channel my father and acknowledge with a low, quiet, deadly "here," but I hadn't hit puberty yet, so a girly squeak came out instead. Often the teacher wouldn't hear me, so she'd say it again, even louder. The laughing and singing wouldn't stop until school ended for the day.

Some of this might've been my fault. If I'd just gone to the teacher beforehand and said I prefer "Rudy" over "Rudolph" during roll maybe it would have solved everything. But I wasn't the sharpest tool in the shed. In fact, I think I was pretty slow, and if not slow, then odd. For example, I remember when my parents bought a new washing machine. It came in a huge box with thick walls and pressed corners. I played in that damn cardboard box for weeks. I sat inside with my used Legos and Hot Wheels, and when that wasn't enough, stole my dad's fix-everything black electrical tape and used it to prevent even a shred of light from coming into the box. The fact that no light was able to enter impressed me for hours.

Five days after moving into the box, I got invited to go see the movie *E.T.* with family friends. For some inexplicable reason, my excitement led me to the idea of bringing a lamp into the box. I turned it on and stared at the light for about three days.

When I emerged, the light was still there, right in front of my face. I could barely see. Later that day, when I went to the movie, I still couldn't see. I squinted my way through it, but I couldn't even make out a single frame. Afterwards, my mom had to take me to the doctor. When I explained to her what I'd done, she seemed more concerned about my brain than my eyes.

A light seemed to go on in my head after that. And it was at around this time, fourth grade or so, when I began to fight back against my fate.

When my dad and I were at the pier on weekends, and he'd hear me getting picked on, his advice was always the same: punch them. Somehow this never appealed to me.

Every day the men pulled in their boats from Kaneohe Bay, and those who came in early cracked open their canned beers and compared their catches. Every day, Brett, another fisherman's son, started in on me. The same old jokes—Rudolph the Red-headed Human, Ronald McDonald, etc.

Brett was everything I wanted to be. He was a tall, dark-haired, tanned boy with spiked hair. He was one of the best surfers and baseball players in our neighborhood. And whether at school or at the pier, he was merciless. The other kids always followed his lead.

So there he was, his face right in mine, jeering away. Punch 'em, my dad had said. But I knew that if I hit Brett, things would turn out badly for me. The other kids were laughing and laughing. All except one: Marshall Trammel. Marshall was, as far as I knew, the only black kid in all of Kahaluu, a dark-skinned African-American who Brett constantly teased.

Just as I was about to slink away, I noticed something.

Brett had bad breath.

I looked at Marshall. "Breath," I said.

The other kids stopped laughing.

I pointed at Brett. "Breath!" I said again.

Marshall took my lead and turned Brett-Breath into an inspired beat-box-filled rap. All the kids were laughing at Brett now. He clenched his fists and started to say something, but changed his mind. He stormed off as a bunch of kids joined in the rap. We were so relentless that on the following Monday, Brett showed up to school with a tiny bottle of Scope in his pocket.

And it continued like this from then on. I certainly still got teased, but I teased back. And if Marshall was with me, we'd wipe the floor with just about anyone. Brett was known as "Breath" from there on out. Another kid with a birthmark on his cheek became "Doodoo cheek." Todd, a big haole kid who was one of the most popular boys in school, became "Buffalo Butt."

I got better and better at it, too. Repetition will do that for you (just about every new kid I met would tease me, so I'd have to tease right back). However, I also knew what it was like to get teased, so I'd normally use insults for defensive purposes only. Through trial and error, I learned it was often effective to act proud of my red hair. For example, when I got older, I'd walk up to female classmates, unprompted, and assure them that the carpet matched the drapes. I also learned that gross-out, one-upmanship humor worked as well. Moon me, and I would give you the finger moon. Then there was just a mountain of silliness that got people laughing. My adamant claims that if you winked at my mom's German Shepherd, Lani, she would wink back. Walking around naked. Playing basketball naked. Apparently naked is funny.

So after the Brett episode, I found myself wanting to make people laugh. And sometimes, for an instant, people would seem to forget that I had red hair. My life drastically improved. I developed a life-long friendship with the only boy I met besides Marshall who didn't tease me: Michael Santos A.K.A. Binky (called that because as a baby, he refused to give up his pacifier). We united because we both constantly got teased (me for my hair, him for his name). He wasn't into teasing other kids, but he'd join me in executing my bright ideas, like the time I tried to build a boat to be like my dad, and it sank the moment Binky and I put it in water.

After I learned how to fight back my way, childhood was good. I still wanted to look like the Bretts of the world, but being able to make people laugh, I discovered, was a more than decent consolation. In fact, my childhood might have even been great, except for one thing: *The Boat*.

2.

Just about all local families in my neighborhood had boats. Some had twenty-footers with leaves filling half the hull, some had half-sunken, fourteen-foot, fiberglass flat-bottoms; what mattered was, they all had boats. And all the boats had stereos. It could be the biggest trash heap of a boat, and sure enough the fish could hear it coming a mile away. Most of the boats had names, too, like " Pua's Pride" or "*Da 'Crazy' Boyz*," and of course "boys" would be spelled with a "z."

Our boat was not like most others. It was a behemoth. A huge sampan cabin cruiser that my dad had built from scratch. He started with a pile of lumber and fiberglass and built a forty-eight foot beauty that slept eight and smelled like low tide.

It was the bane of my existence.

All my friends used to tease me because they knew all my extra time and weekends went to cleaning that boat. I scrubbed that boat and cleaned those bilges more times than I want to remember. The good news was that boat taught me how to work with my hands, which became useful later in life. It also taught me that hard work is good for you. Hard, physical labor was the common commodity known to all local families. If you worked hard, you were doing well. If you worked harder than others, people knew it and respected you for it. The problem was, or so I thought at the time, most local people knew how to work harder but not smarter.

It was this concept of working smarter that made laboring on The Boat difficult for me in the beginning. I was always a dreamer trying to think up ways to make even simple tasks easier. I did this a lot around the boat. When my little inventions didn't work out, however, it was my dad who paid the price. The perfect example is the time I built a contraption to hold a flashlight.

You see, the boat's engine compartment could either hold ten of me or one of my dad. It sat under the main cabin and was four feet below the floor board. The four-by-four heavy floor board was carpeted with a dark brown Berber carpet. This carpet was most likely recalled off the market years prior due to its unique ability to hold an odor and cause a rash. Dad loved it because it never looked dirty. Under this carpeted cover was the beginning of a labyrinth that I knew all too well. It led to the huge, green, Detroit diesel engine.

Contained in this maze was an array of criss-crossing wooden beams that filled most of the passageways into the aft of the ship. Each beam was completely covered in a thick layer of mildew and oil. Further down, a bilge pump worked surrounded by a constant pool of black, oily water. "Don't step on the pump! You going break um!" my dad would say.

You would think it was made of glass the way he obsessed about this thing. But if it was so precious, couldn't he have found a better place for the pump? It was directly in the middle of our path, and its location assured that we were going to get dirty because we had to cling to the sides of the oil-encrusted space to make sure that we didn't touch the holy pump.

Aft of the pump was a large opening for the diesel engine, which was supported by rotted two-by-fours and rusted metal brackets. Covered in muck, I would lay in this confined space for hours. I knew first hand what those little white lab rats scurrying through mazes feel like. It didn't matter how short the expedition into this land of oil and grime was, when I emerged I was always covered in a layer of impenetrable black slime. This is when I found out that my dad and everyone else at the pier loved or should I say worshiped this one kind of gritty orange degreasing paste.

"Ho! You got to use da orange stuff braddah! Something about the citric enzyme acids!"

I never quite got the name of the stuff because the bottle was always covered with grease. Even brand-new bottles would come smudged with filth; it was probably a promotional gimmick. Anyway, at least it worked to get me clean, and so far I'm cancer free.

Regardless, whenever the job was too big for me to pull off, my dad had to get out the giant shoehorn and squeeze himself into that hole. This meant it was now my job to hold the flashlight.

I would lie on that itchy, musty carpet and hold that light for hours. Occasionally my dad would look up at me and shoot me an "at-a boy" and that would carry me for several hours more. One bright afternoon, after holding that light for three hours, I came up with one of my ideas.

It was a glorious day. The bay flat, the water clean enough to see crabs scurry on the ocean bottom, and here I was stuck in this boat. At my age, I just wanted to be outside playing in the water. Seconds felt like eternities, and while I held that flashlight, I knew something had to be done. It was immediately after an "at-a boy" when I sprang into action. My father had two green metal ammunition cases the size of shoe boxes filled with nuts, bolts, washers and screws—all rusty. I still remember the sound of us digging through those metal containers. A dull, rhythmic scraping that was pleasant until about thirty seconds later when dad would just pour it all out. Funny, when he dumped it out, the nut we needed was usually staring us in the face at the top of the pile. "We'll just clean that up later," Dad would say. In other words, I'd be cleaning it up later by myself.

This time around, the box had been dumped, so I decided to engineer a tool made of bolts, fishing wire, and spoons that could hold this damn light. It took me about forty-five minutes, working one-handed, which was pretty impressive considering the light beam never deviated from my father's target during construction. When I was done, I snuck away and figured I had a good hour before the next "at-a boy." In the meantime, he wouldn't even notice I was gone. About twenty minutes later, I was on the bow of the boat throwing my dad's rusty screws at the fish when the inevitable happened.

"Shit! Rudy Boy!"

So I wasn't an engineer; hell, I was only twelve. My invention had experienced a total catastrophic structural meltdown. Design flaw or defective material—maybe I used too many screws and not enough fishing line. The little lighthouse had toppled on my dad. I was terrified. I knew my dad was hot from being in that hole for hours. I immediately ran to him and apologized. Fortunately, he was crammed in that hole, and it would take too much energy to get out and wring my neck, so I had time to plead my case.

"I was trying to work smarter not harder."

He paused. He looked at me curiously and said, "Stop playing around. Don't be lazy."

Shockingly, that was it and he went back to work. He didn't rage for once. Maybe he was too tired to climb out of that hole to show me how it felt to have a two-pound flashlight crash on my head. But I think it was something else. Maybe as a man who built boats from scratch, no blue prints, no computer generated models, just a napkin with a banana-shaped sketch on it with "48" in parentheses, maybe he saw a bit of himself in his red-headed son for the first time.

Regardless, and this was to my utter dismay, Dad always eventually got out of that damn engine box and the boat would be fixed. Because there was something worse than holding that damn light: going out on the boat. Yes, now it was time to go fishing. Great for him, bad for me. I got deathly seasick. We're talking gut-wrenching puke splatters that smelled of ginger, spices, or whatever old wives' voodoo remedy that I'd taken to help prevent the inevitable.

The boat was my personal torture chamber. My reward for spending all my free time fixing the constant leaks and oily bilges was to get the honor of puking for twelve hours straight every Saturday. Fishing trips always started the same way. We would pull up to the pier at what felt like zero o'clock in the morning. We would load the boat with the day's supplies. After the boat was packed with ice, food, equipment, and beer, the ropes were thrown to the dock, and we started that slow trek out of the protection of Heeia Kea harbor. My place for the next few hours, until we reached the fishing grounds, would be on top of the engine box. I would lay on that engine box, on the diesel-heated, brown Berber carpet that emanated the smell of salt and fish, awaiting the bile to flood my mouth. I would dig in and try to fall asleep as fast as I could.

With the huge engine purring, with its slow and constant vibration, the box was always comfortable at first, even sooth-ing, for awhile. Unfortunately, after an hour, the sandpaper texture of the carpet would chaff my skin raw and wake me up. Then I would lay there trying not to move or think of food for fear of intense heaves. How I hated it. The only time I didn't was in that hour or two right at the beginning of the trip when the carpet didn't burn me, and I wasn't puking my toenails up.

Sometimes as we'd make our way further and further out to sea, Mrs. Conan's sixth grade history lesson would come to mind. On November 28th 1520, Magellan and a crew of 270 men rounded Cape Horn and entered a serene ocean, which he named the Pacific, for its calm and peacefulness. Who knew that the great Portuguese explorer could be so stupid. He was probably the same comedian who named Greenland and Iceland, too. It was my personal theory that he was the sole reason why Portagees got such a bad rap in Hawaii.

It was never subtle, the ride out. Even with my eyes closed, I knew exactly when we'd hit the head buoy and were out into the open, "calm" Pacific Ocean. Once we passed the buoy, out of the shelter of the jetty and outside reef, the great north and east swells would start to converge on our now unprotected vessel. The moment we passed Mokumanu Island I would immediately feel the sway of the boat change. The gentle bay waters quickly turned into a memory. A continuous cadence of lunges forwarded the boat.

My dad's motto: The rougher the better. The fish can't see the fishing line so good. My motto: one hand on the boat, the other hand on the bucket.

The seas we would venture out in were formidable. For my dad, small craft warning meant: I hope it picks up a little. The boat chugged up swell faces fifteen to twenty feet high. At first, there would be a slight incline in our attitude while the engine would slightly strain as the big diesel drove us up the swell. The boat would then lunge forward with an audible drain in the engine's revolutions and our pitch became extreme. For a moment it would feel as if the boat had lost ground and retreated before it would crash violently into the trough of the next oncoming wave. Propellers would spin over the surface of the water for a second and a loud "whoosh" would herald the next oncoming swell.

During all this, my father just stared straight ahead, bobbing side-to-side and up-and-down in his captain's chair. Soaked from head-to-toe, he never squinted or showed an ounce of worry. For him it was probably like being in his father's truck as a kid. Dust and asbestos swirling throughout the cab, Pops refusing to acknowledge their existence. Now my dad was like him, too. I, on the other hand, huddled and grabbed for anything that was nailed down.

This was only the start of a very long day. The sequence of events would then go as follows: First, a little tingle. Then a burst of saliva would fill my mouth. It was my body's way of greasing the runway. Then I would have my trusty 10w-30 yellow Pennzoil bucket ready to go.

Then I puked. And puked. Then puked some more.

After I was sure I spewed out everything I'd eaten within the last month, I would look at the outriggers and pray to God that a fish wouldn't strike. I felt like the only person in the history of Hawaiian culture who ever pleaded with the ocean to not let a fish bite. But my father was too damn good; this was his trade, after all. He would sometimes see birds or rubbish from so far away that I used to think he got his information from NASA. And eventually, sure enough, hanapaa! The yelling and screaming started.

I knew the drill. I would be in my sick-to-my-stomach stupor, the sun beating on the deck, and everything was sharp, hot, and salty. Even the wind would mock me. It would whirl around the back of the boat so the fumes of diesel exhaust would waft past my face. It was Dante's undiscovered level of hell. At this point, my body was programmed; I was nothing but a robot. My role was plain as day. First, I had to clear all the lines, which sounds easy, but in my condition, was pure anguish.

The reels were like large winches, and the fine line that encircled the spool was a tangle ready to happen. If I stared at the reel too long, I would puke again. But if I didn't concentrate, I would tangle everything. As much as I hated it, I knew that I could never let my sickness stand in the way of catching fish. This was my family's income. So I just puked on the reels while I worked.

After the lines were clear, my thumb chaffed bloody from guiding in six reels, my next job was to get out of the way. My father had an interesting way of fishing. Dad would furiously reel the fish halfway to the boat just to figure out what type of fish was on the line, then he would tell me to take the reel. Sounds important, but all I really was doing was taking up the slack. Once my dad determined that a fish was worthy, he would return to hand-haul the fish into the boat.

For years, whenever I happened to watch a television fishing program—and I was, perversely, a fan—showing those heroic haole dudes strapped in fighting chairs reeling in marlin, all I could think was: pussies.

Dad's method: no gloves or fancy fighting chairs, just forearms and years of built-up calluses. To be clear, yes, hand-lining means grabbing the fishing line and pulling in the sometimes half-a-ton fish *with his hands*. He would toy with fish more than twice his size. He knew when to give the fish slack and when to start horsing it in. It was uncanny. Like a conductor, he would sway his arms up and down with the cadence of the rocking boat while he walked back and forth.

It was all very rhythmical. Sometimes I squinted to make the fishing line disappear, just to see Dad waltzing with an invisible partner.

Dad had taught hand-lining to many friends. Some lost fingers. "Too much hurry," Dad would say. Whether they lost a finger on the right or left hand, he always called them lefty.

Anyway, once I had cleared the lines, I'd watch my dad haul eight-hundred to a thousand-pound marlins to the boat. I would watch him as I reeled in the slack. It all seems impressive now, but honestly, back then, when he wrapped his bare hands around the fishing line, I would think: idiot.

I'm sorry, but I didn't care; I was just trying not to barf. Yet I have to admit that once the fish got close enough to see, the entire ordeal seemed almost worth it.

When the fish would get closer, it was a beautiful sight, especially the mahi-mahi.

"Look she stay yellow and tired! Grab the gaff!" my dad would yell.

It would snap me out of my haze. It was amazing to see this magnificent fish visually signaling to us that it was done fighting. That it would rather die than fight anymore. The sight was also depressing to me as a kid.

However mixed my feelings, I would only witness nature's losing battle for a brief second before the water was filled with blood from my dad's flying gaff. That man could gaff a manini in the perfect spot at ten paces every time. The gaff would be lodged tight behind the head with blood spilling from the sides of the over-sized stainless steel hook. He would then haul the fish into the boat with a giant heave and grab his Louisville Slugger. He'd hit that fish like a pinata. After bludgeoning the fish to death, we hosed the blood and regurgitated bait fish from the deck. I would then return to my place on the engine box and continue to pray for no more fish.

You would think that after a few years of this, I would have stood up and said, "Enough!" But who was I going to complain to and what was I going to say? "I feel sick. Can I go home to mom and help her knit?"

How could I say this to a man who had once got bitten on the leg by a giant ono at seven in the morning and then continued to fish until five because he'd "never seen so much rubbish in the water." When Dad finally got back to shore and went to the emergency room, the doctor sewed seventy-three stitches in his leg. This was after it had taken the nurse an hour to sterilize the area; Dad had stopped the bleeding by wrapping his leg with his all-purpose black electrical tape.

There was no way around it. I couldn't wimp out.

Long story short, we had this particular boat for several years, which, by the way was named after my sister, Kathy. Because Kathy weighed 7 pounds 11 ounces at birth, the fuss couldn't have been greater if she'd been born with a birthmark of Jesus Christ on her chest.

"Ho! Seven eleven, we go Vegas!"

I heard that about a million times growing up. Kathy still hears it.

Anyway, back to Kathy, the boat not the sister. It sank. Not so lucky after all. Well, not for everyone that is. Me, I felt like I hit the lottery. The boat sank and my dad was lost at sea. Honestly, this might sound insensitive, but I really didn't worry too much. I remember my mom and sisters freaking out, running around the house and calling everyone who owned even a row boat to help them search for him. I, on the other hand, knew my dad a bit better. Heaven didn't want him and hell was scared of him. I *knew* he would be back. Unlike my mom and sisters, I had been out on that boat with him countless times. I imagined him fashioning a rudimentary lathe and constructing a primitive pulley system made out of chopsticks and a rubber band that would propel him back home. Seriously though, that man was nails. So when he and my uncle were found forty miles outside of Kaneohe Bay, bobbing on a cooler in the middle of eighteen-foot swells, it was no big surprise to me.

The only thing that surprised me was the cooler wasn't filled with fish.

....

I'd been admitted on a Monday night, pumped full of the experimental drug, Xigris, on Tuesday. Most of what happened on the rest of that day and all of Wednesday was a blur. It was now Thursday, and Lynn told me I was getting better. At first, I didn't believe it. I still felt awful, couldn't talk, had a tough time breathing. Besides, even if the strep pneumo didn't get me, there were other dangers lurking. For example, I'd been sedentary for so long that a possible pulmonary embolism was a concern. But I was alive. And I was scared again. In retrospect, a good sign.

In fact, later that Thursday, I was moved out of ICU—forty pounds lighter. Though I didn't think of it then because I was too exhausted to think. Now when I re-live those days in the hospital, I remember critical care survival rates. When I'd worked in the shock trauma unit in Houston and when I headed the critical care unit at MD Anderson, death was, for the most part, predictable. Tally up an Apache score, and the percent calculated predicted the odds of survival accurately for the most part. However, as a rule, an Apache score never reached 100%. There was no certainty, and the score reflected this.

Besides Apache scores, we came up with a handful of non-scientific mortality predictors. Of course, people who gave up survived less than those who fought. Jerks tended to survive while really nice people seemed more predisposed to death in trauma. Gang-bangers often seemed to have an almost supernatural resistance to should-be-fatal gunshot wounds. Wives of lawyers tended to fare far worse in critical care than the general public. Doctors, too. I have no idea why. Like I said, unscientific.

Then there were the one-in-a-million cases, the ones that frustrated and perplexed doctors to no end. An eighty-year-old woman on life support after having half a lung and most of her intestines removed, awake the next day. An otherwise vigorous eighteen-year-old who stopped breathing after one round of chemo. There was one patient we had, Mon Dragon. "The Dragon," we called him. A gunshot victim. We had to take out half his liver. Then he caught pneumonia. We treated that. Then he developed a foot ulcer that got infected. We treated that. Then he developed an allergic reaction to medication. We switched medicines and stabilized him. Each new ailment that popped up almost killed him.

The Dragon was in our critical care unit for nine months. He seemed immortal. After almost a year, when he was finally sitting up and talking, we were all giving each other high fives.

My case was not as incredible as The Dragon's. However, when I was moved out of ICU, the fact that I had an awful Apache score (less than one percent chance of survival), the fact that I gave up, the fact that I was a pretty nice guy, and the fact that I was a doctor should have meant almost certain death. To this day, I have no idea how I survived.

However, what am I going to do, complain? When I look back, it seems like I'd always been lucky. If I'd grown up during my father's or older sisters' era, I doubt I would have become a doctor. If I didn't go to the high school I attended and met the friends that I did, my life may have turned out differently as well. If diesel fuel prices hadn't skyrocketed when they did, I would have probably ended up being a mechanic instead of a doctor.

However, when prone on a hospital bed, tubes sticking out of me and barely conscious, I wasn't thinking of myself as Mr. Lucky. I was waiting for disaster to strike. I figured the bill had finally come due. I'd spent a decent chunk of my younger days pushing my luck. Pitch black night diving and the light goes out. Shrugging and taking my best guess as to which direction I had to swim to get to shore. Blasting around town in my beater Honda Civic. Once, a couple of friends and I thought it it'd be fun to race from Aloha Stadium to Manoa. Needle almost buried, I tried to take the hairpin University Avenue cut-off and slammed into barrels filled with sand. The sand exploded in front of the windshield, and for a moment, I thought I was seeing my life dissolve.

Riding motorcycle as a kid. Taking the H-3 home just to see how fast I could go. One badly-placed pebble, and they would've had to shovel me into the back of an ambulance. Shutting down the power on a single-engine airplane that was worth about as much as my piece-of-crap Honda Civic. Gliding at eight thousand feet. One bone-headed move and there wouldn't have been anything to shovel. I'd pushed my luck so often that when I was about to be carted from ICU, I actually visualized the blood clot with my name on it, heading to my lungs, embolism imminent. After a sickly childhood and all the dumb risks I'd taken throughout life, disaster was my due.

Weak and in pain, my discomfort and fear turned to anger, a male Puana tradition. I wanted everyone out. I demanded that my sister Kathy and my parents fly back home. I wanted to murder the nurse who had woken me up to give me a sleeping pill. I told Lynn that I wanted the Foley, a catheter that went up my urethra into my bladder, out of me. I didn't think about it at the time, but perhaps my being a jerk upped my chances of survival. Like I said, jack asses tend to fare better than nice people in hospitals.

All my youthful bone-headed lack of awareness of death was gone. I wasn't immortal anymore. I feared for my life during every second of consciousness. Looking back at it now, I'm surprised psychologists haven't come up with some kind of fear/anger formula. One hour of constant fear equals petrified. One day equals tear-streak fatigue. After two days of constant fear, you just want death to pop out of your chest like a jack-in-the-box so you can punch him in his face. But after dropping forty pounds in several days, I didn't have the strength for that. As far as I was concerned, I was just another Puana hanging onto a cooler in the midst of eighteen-foot swells, only no one was going to come rescue me.

Chapter Three

Opio (Youth)

When it came time for my parents to choose a high school for me, public was out of the question. Public school would've meant Castle High in Kaneohe. I knew more people who went to Castle and didn't graduate than people who did.

My parents were already scrimping, saving, and struggling to pay for Kathy's private school tuition. My dad worked full-time at Pearl Harbor then fished on the weekends for money. My mom sold her antique jewelry to pay for private school books. What they didn't want us to become was what they called "typical Hawaiians." To them, there were two types of typical Hawaiians. Those who smoked ice at bus stops and had given up on life before they even tried. Then there were those who embraced the Hawaiian culture and waved protest signs. I'm not sure which type of typical Hawaiians my parents disliked more. None of us kids were allowed to apply to Kamehameha Schools—a Hawaiian-only prep school that was the richest in the state and hardly charged tuition.

"That is where all the stupid activists go."

"They just need to learn to shut up."

"They make shame for the rest of us."

My parents grew up in a different era. It wasn't like today with the "imua" and "kau inoa" mentality. There was no pride, no immersion schools, no desire to resurrect a dying culture. Back then, when my parents were coming of age, many Hawaiians were ashamed of being Hawaiian, and my father was no exception. Both of them were taught to eat pain and tragedy. Be stoic even if you lose everything. They did not understand protest culture. By the time the Civil Rights and anti-war movements got rolling in the sixties, they were already living on a pig farm and struggling to support a growing family. To them, protesters were of the weakest sort. They were complainers—the worst thing you could be in my parents' eyes.

So for my education, they settled on the same school my sister Kathy attended, one of the most expensive and easiest to get into in the state: Mid-Pacific Institute.

Mid-Pac was in Manoa Valley, a far drive from Kahaluu, and among its student body were heirs to contracting, soda, and shampoo empires. There were a ton of Asian students, but among the rest, there was a decent mix. If Punahou was the haole school, and Iolani was the smart Japanese school, Mid-Pac was sort of the in-between; it was also the place where kids went if they couldn't get into Punahou or Iolani. While Punahou graduated the founder of AOL and a President of the United States, and Iolani counted a mayor, a movie studio head, a MacArthur Prize winner, and some guy named Sun Yat-sen among its alumni, Mid-Pac graduated minor actors, businessmen, and one Chief Justice of the Hawaii State Supreme Court. Certainly many students who graduated from Mid-Pac enjoyed success, but none had names that truly rang out.

Cliques in Mid-Pac were very much race-based. The Japanese kids (and there were a ton of Japanese kids who didn't get into Iolani) hung out together. One Japanese group cruised in dropped mini-trucks, their rims, car stereos, and hydraulic truck beds paid for by Mom and Dad. The baseball players, mostly Japanese as well and from suburbs like Aiea and Pearl

City, partied together after games on weekends. Most of the Filipinos and Chinese joined the Japanese cliques (this may partially be why I remember there being so many Japanese students). Then there were the haoles—the acting clique, the surf clique, the stoner clique, and the party clique. There were also a few token Hawaiians sprinkled here and there—some into hula and sports, and the rest who did their own thing. Hawaiians did join cliques based on common interest. In other words, there'd be one Hawaiian partying with ten or so Japanese mini-truck Waikiki cruisers or one among the baseball players. As the pale-skinned, red-headed Hawaiian, I had no idea what group to join. At first this was a source of anxiety and confusion, but then I realized, as the boy who could pass as haole, as the boy, who if you looked closely enough could pass as Hawaiian, and as a football player, I had a lot of choices.

There were two brothers, Andy and Chris, who as far as I knew, were the only other Mid-Pac students from Kahaluu besides me and my sister Kathy. They were among the first friends I made at Mid-Pac. Andy was a mini-truck guy. Chris hung out with the baseball guys. Then there was Todd, a big haole from Kaneohe who went to the same elementary school as me (the same Todd who we'd called "Buffalo Butt"). By the time we were in high school, he was a gifted offensive lineman and class president. Sometimes I spent time with him and a couple of the haole cliques. My sister Kathy, who was dating the all-state high school baseball player of the year at the time, let me hang out with the older kids as well.

Did people tease about my hair and my name when I started school at Mid-Pac? Sure. But by then, I had been trained to fight back. The Asian kids were particularly easy targets. Let's just say that there was a noticeable difference in the size of one body part that that did not go unnoticed in the football locker room. Tease my hair, and I would tease your shortcomings.

Up to this point, all my life I wanted to be Hawaiian or local-looking. But for the first time I was embracing my red-headed Hawaiian identity. I was voted class clown and made many good friends. However, there were consequences to my sudden popularity.

Kathy and I were basically failing out of high school. And my father was pissed. The poor guy was slaving away seven-days-a-week to pay for a prep school that he could not afford, for an education my mom insisted on, and it was being wasted on a couple of lazy, ungrateful kids. (It didn't help that my two other older sisters, who had attended Star of the Sea, another expensive private school, had hardly been scholars.) But every-one knew Mom ruled the roost. Dad could be as kolohe as he wanted so long as that paycheck came every week. She put up with a lot of drunken nights and adolescent escapades to pro-tect us.

Anyway, Dad gave Mom money, Mom paid tuition and did her best to hide the fact that we all sucked in school. Kathy and I would have won the prize for closest to failing but didn't. It was crazy how anybody, but especially my Dad, could shell out so much money for something and not really know how we were doing in it. Mom was like the CEO of Enron; she cooked the books something fierce. She knew if my dad ever saw my report card, he would kill me. So she gave him his allowance and hid our grades to keep the peace. Mom saved our butts, and we survived to slack another day.

Every one of my high school teachers would tell you I was hardly the next Einstein. I was a joker who never took classes seriously. I would party and get drunk with the townies on the weekends and go diving with my Kahaluu friends on the weekdays. School was just a big time setback. Besides, as a Hawaiian, I was pigeon-holed anyway. My social studies teacher straight up told me that I would never be able to live in Kahala (an affluent neighborhood on Oahu) with the last name "Puana."

My response: "Who would want to live in Kahala? It's too hot and filled with haoles."

Anyway, I didn't care. I wasn't going to college anyway. With my grades and SAT scores, I assumed I couldn't even get into the University of Hawaii. So I was hell-bent on going to diesel mechanic school after graduation. The Boat's diesel engine was the only thing I really enjoyed on those long weekends fishing. I idolized how my dad could fix anything. I liked taking something broken and making it go again. I was good with my hands and as my dad always said, "Well, you sure aren't scared of getting dirty." So I thought diesel mechanic school would be a natural fit.

However, something happened the year I was suppose to squeak past graduation day.

With the help of another B in art to offset the D in history, I was ready to graduate from high school. In eight months, I was set to join one of the dozens of expanding diesel mechanic schools throughout the country. Then, like a bolt of lightning, diesel went from a little over fifty-cents-a-gallon to over a dollar-and-seventy. It more than tripled practically overnight. This crippled the world of diesel; car companies stopped making diesel cars, generator manufacturers switched to gas engines. And that is what closed a lot of the trade schools. The remaining schools actually became selective, and now there was no way I could get in with my grades. I was sickened; all of a sudden I had no future. Moreover, even if I could get in at some time in the future, what was the point? Diesel was over.

Reluctantly, I decided to shoot for college. And, to my surprise, at first college seemed much easier to get into. Of course, diesel mechanic schools were not interested in any minority blood quantum. College was a different story.

It was Mom who found this out. Overwrought about my future, she frantically searched for a way to get me into the University of Hawaii. And my Hawaiian Blood quantum did help, but my grades were so bad it was hardly a done deal. That's when Mom dug deeper and found a summer program that would take me: Blue Water Marine Laboratories. If I finished this program, UH would let me in.

So there we were, a bunch of underachievers trapped on a boat in the middle of the Pacific for three months. Sprinkle some seaweed on us, and poof, you got scholars. And it was great: imagine a boat full of girls trapped at sea with only a handful of guys. Luckily, my seasickness had been gone for years. After all my sea voyages with Dad, the center in my brain that induced motion sickness finally gave up and died. Now you could put me in a blender and I would come out reading a newspaper and eating a pastrami sandwich.

I met my first serious girlfriend that summer. She got me through the program then eventually left me for a big, handsome stranger: the Mainland.

But I finished the program and was off to college the following Fall.

2.

A good friend of mine often laments the era in which we grew up. As Generation X-ers, we missed out on Flower Power, Free Love, The Beatles, punk, and the excesses of the 70's. We preceded Google, *Girls Gone Wild*, sexting, and smart phones. As children of the 80's we got AIDS, Just Say No, MTV, and A Flock of Seagulls. We still had to raid our fathers' hidden stashes of *Playboy* to see naked women, and as young adults, we grew mullets, pierced our ears, and carried around pagers. Sad days indeed.

In some ways, it was even worse to be a Gen X-er in Hawaii. During childhood, we were still a week behind the Mainland when it came to TV, and three years behind when it came to just about everything else. We were too young to remember days when the beaches weren't packed with tourists and when the fishing was easy, the days when my father didn't have to head out forty miles to sea to fish. And as adults, we would be the first generation to face paying half-a-million dollars for forty-year-old single-story houses in middle-of-nowhere suburbs just to hang on in Hawaii.

It was, however, a good time to be in college. Suddenly, being Hawaiian was popular. The greats of the Second Hawaiian Renaissance (people like Gabby Pahinui, the Beamers, Nainoa Thompson, and Eddie Aikau) paved the way and made it cool to be kanaka maoli. There was even a new Hawaiian Studies program at the University of Hawaii. Unlike my father, who endured racism growing up, who was, despite his amazing ingenuity (remember, he built huge boats from scratch with zero schooling or instruction), pigeon-holed into a working-class existence, the college Hawaiians of my generation were embraced, encouraged, and even emulated. It was not uncommon to meet haoles and Asians walking around campus who'd adorned themselves with fanciful Hawaiian names. A white guy named Sam was now Kamuela. A Japanese named David was born again as Kawika. Those blonde twins Kaimiloa and Kawika danced hula, tattooed their new names on their backs, and took Hawaiian language classes. If my dad had gone to college with me, he head would have probably exploded. But as the real red-haired thing, I felt right at home.

I started college as a dormer, living in Wainani, a three-story, on-campus student walk-up with two-bedroom, one-bath apartments that housed four students each. My first roommate was Ben, a big, teddybear Samoan. My second was Marc, a good friend from high school. Chris, who'd left home and was still in high school, was a permanent fixture. Andy, who'd left home as well and was living with his girlfriend, attended Kapiolani Community College. He was always around, too.

My new friends were mostly Hawaiian and, like me, had barely made it into UH. Kealii and Kaniau—both eighteen-years-old and over two-fifty easy—looked like a professional wrestling tag team. We called them Mauna Loa and Mauna Kea. Then there was Dominic and Layton, one a dark-skinned Hawaiian who was built like a TV lifeguard, the other, a graduate of Kamehameha, who was as big as Kealii and Kaniau and a math genius to boot. He was the only math genius I'd ever met who always walked around in busted-up tee-shirts and jeans stained with latex paint.

There were others. Hawaiian Ryan, from Waianae, who was a bouncer at Bobby McGee's. Shane, a half-Hawaiian, half-Japanese kid from Kona who sang and played the ukulele better than anyone else at the dorms. The poor guy had to teach over a dozen people how to play the uke, including me, Chris, and Andy.

For what felt like the first time in history, Hawaiians found each other and created bonds in an institution of higher learning. It was amazing. And being the red-headed Hawaiian was no longer a liability. Everyone embraced it, even loved it. I was proud to be the *only* one.

Needless to say, we partied. We picked up girls. We played our ukuleles and slurred Hawaiian lyrics most of us could not even translate. We filled our cups with kegged beer. (Mauna Loa and Mauna Kea used empty gallon wine jugs instead of cups.) Hung over, we skipped classes and played Nintendo instead.

We also made an enemy. Steve, our resident advisor, was the type of haole who overcompensated and tried to be more Hawaiian than the Hawaiians. He paddled canoe, took Hawaiian language classes, and had a Hawaiian tattoo with a made-up Hawaiian name on his back. He always wore some Hawaiian trinket around his neck like a shark's tooth or a koa hook. I guess we were supposed to believe this guy swam with sharks and knew how to use that hook. He wore a long, brown pony tail. Somehow even the pony tail was condescending.

But the most irritating thing about Steve was his attempts at speaking pidgin. People who didn't grow up with it just don't have it. When Steve used to come over and talk to our friends, they would all just laugh. This pissed him off because he thought he was fooling everyone with his Milwaukee accent and a lava-lava wrapped around his waist.

On top of our friends thinking he was a joke, Steve lived right next to us and had to deal with our parties. That I looked more haole than him and had a huge group of Hawaiian friends seemed to infuriate him, as did breaking up parties he wasn't invited to. He was brave, though. I give him credit. It took balls to tell a bunch of Hawaiians from Waianae, Kalihi, and Waimanalo to pack it up for the night. They didn't listen, of course, but I had to respect the man. And, really, the biggest reason why Marc and I didn't invite him was that we were protecting him. Townie locals at paddling practice were a lot more tolerant than moke country Hawaiians. We knew what would have happened if Steve attended a party. He would have a few drinks and get comfortable. He would tell our friends about his canoe paddling practice and why he chose his Hawaiian name. He would then start to butcher pidgin and the Hawaiian language, telling everyone he was Hawaiian at heart. And that would be about it. He would've gotten stomped.

Little did we know, there were a tidal wave of Steves coming to Hawaii. At this point, if you live near the beach, chances are you know at least one.

Anyway, things went on like this for a year. We partied, skipped class, and were put on academic probation—typical college stuff. We gained weight (for Hawaiians the "freshman fifteen" can easily turn into a "freshman thirty"), and our personal hygiene was utterly disgusting. As someone who grew up hopelessly dependant on a mother and three older sisters, not only was I the only red-headed Hawaiian, but I was also renowned for the grossest on-campus student resident. My stained twin mattress never bore a sheet. I never did laundry. I'd sometimes stuff my underwear in Marc's dirty clothes and laugh and laugh as he pulled my BVD's out of his now clean pockets. Clean towels? Sometimes I'd actually dry myself off with the bathroom floor mat. When that grossed even me out,

I started to air dry on the balcony outside. Steve just loved that. At one point during freshman year we acquired a maggot problem. My friends would watch with wonder as I nonchalantly swept them up with an old magazine.

This lack of self-respect and responsibility extended to other things as well. For example, neither Marc or I realized that we had a mailbox. So for one year, we never checked the mail. We didn't even ask ourselves why we didn't receive any mail for a year. Our mothers took care of that kind of stuff when we'd lived at home.

So at the end of freshman year, when Steve informed us that we had two boxes of mail waiting for us downstairs, we didn't believe him. We demanded that he show us this fictional mailbox. We walked downstairs, and sure enough, there it was. I then realized what that little key was for that they'd given me at the beginning of the school year.

Among the two boxes of envelopes was our dorm renewal application. The due date had long expired. This would be our first and last year as college dormers.

Steve had gotten his revenge.

............3.

Fortunately for all of us, Chris enrolled in UH the following semester and scored a dorm room in Noelani—the on-campus apartments right next to Wainani. So in essence, though we lost our room, we all became part-time dormers, only this time around, it was us instead of Chris on the couch. In May, when his roommates would return home for the summer, he housed

me, Marc, Hawaiian Ryan and Waipa. It was a free for all fight
for beds during those months.

The parties resumed. Kealii and Kaniau would pound three-
day-old raw oysters that we'd brought back from our Mokuleia
camping trips and wash them down with jugs of beer. Hawaiian
Ryan would jump on his moped and make runs to Jack-in-
the-Box and return with twenty ninety-nine cent Jumbo Jacks.
Once we turned twenty-one, our friend Brandon would raid his
mother's giant coin jar so he could buy drinks at Moose Mc-
Gillycuddy's in Puck's Alley. I became the shotgun king since
I could open my throat better than anyone else, all because of
the puking I had done on the boat as a kid. Fastest time: 1.2
seconds.

We made new friends as well. Craig, a Kamehameha grad,
who had a stellar academic record until he took Math 100 with
Chris. It was the first and only D he received in college. There
were the Japanese Maui guys, Scott and Wade, and their roommate Reid. The Waipahu Filipino, Mario. And sometimes Andy
and Chris's cousins would show up: Jeff, who was a Golden
Gloves boxer as a kid, and John, a master car and motorcycle
thief who would spend his twenty-first birthday in prison. In
fact, he would go on to spend most of his birthdays in prison
after that as well.

There were summer jobs. The first summer, I was a private
eye's assistant for my old friend Todd's dad. The second summer, Marc and I worked for a furniture moving company that
never moved furniture. Instead we stripped electrical wires and
built cubicles. Just about all the other employees were chronics.
Funny, because one of our biggest contracts had us on-site at
the building of the new Honolulu Police Department head-
quarters. The job also included scheduled nap times and a trip

to Guam (a hot, miserable Hawaii with the same problems, only worse infrastructure and health care). Marc and I met the most connected elevator repair guy there. He had the contracts for every elevator on Guam. Drove around that tiny island in a Lamborghini.

So other than summers, there we were in college, most of our group Hawaiian, the sons of blue-collar fathers who'd never finished high school. At heart we felt we were supposed to be like our dads, be rough-and-tumble, party hard, and reenact the crazy stories of their youths. But what never occurred to us was that our fathers had earned this behavior after they completed mind-numbing, back-breaking ten-hour shifts working with their hands day after day. For us, there were no ten-hour shifts, just an unsupervised slackfest, and we skipped straight to the partying. One-by-one, my friends either dropped out or got kicked out of college. Kaniau knocked up his girlfriend, got married, and left school. Kealii, not sure what happened, but last I heard he was cleaning grease traps at public elementary schools. Layton—MIA. Hawaiian Ryan—MIA. Not sure if they finished. Another of our friends dropped out, went back home to Waianae, and shot himself a few months later.

After the first two years of college, as friends disappeared I found myself hanging out with criminal John more than anyone else, doing things that could get me arrested. I started getting burnt out. I started to ask, was my high school social studies teacher right, was it impossible for a guy with the last name "Puana" to grow up, get a good job, and live in a neighborhood like Kahala (since for him, apparently living in Kahala symbolized the pinnacle of success)? Were we Hawaiian students, most of us the first generation of our families to attend college, pigeon-holed just like our fathers, destined to drop out of school, work construction, become alcoholics, and collect workman's comp after on-the-job injury? Was I wasting my time?

The answer, of course, was yes. I was wasting my time. Instead of attending classes, I was going on adventures with John, even though my red hair, especially in the dead of night, was a liability and would probably get me arrested sooner or later. Instead of studying, I was trying to beat my beer shotgun record time of 1.2 seconds. Instead of thinking about the future, I was mindlessly jeopardizing it.

I was hitting rock bottom. And oddly, it was the combination of a daytime soap opera and a cynical, wise-ass friend that turned things around.

4.

Yet another inebriated night. It was November 23, 1993. Chris and I were on the couch in his dorm room. Even though I was technically now living back at home in Kahaluu, I was permanently camped out on Chris's beer-stained couch. We were both hung chowder with that feeling that we either had to open another beer or suffer through a headache. To top it off, a few hours earlier, we had made a run to Hungry Lion Inn. The Hungry Lion was a twenty-four hour diner in Nuuanu that had been built around a banyan tree. The tree trunk was actually in the middle of the restaurant, and the ambience was further enhanced by Muzak that played bird chirping sounds on loop. Even now, I can still see the saliva coming off of Chris's lip as he slurred to the waitress "Aloha Bowl peese."

Aloha Bowl was a mix of local favorites—a mound of rice covered with a hamburger patty, roast pork, chicken katsu, and curry. It was a mess, but the Aloha Bowl was the perfect man food. For us, man food had two rules. One, no woman under one-hundred-and-eighty pounds would ever order it unless they were sharing it with a guy; and two, it only tasted good when you were drunk. Trust me, we'd tried it sober several times and grossed out.

Anyway, back on the couch. We were both hungover and watching, of all things, *General Hospital*.

Luke and Laura. The Scorpios. Frisco and Felicia Jones. It was Chris who had introduced all of us to the world or Port Charles, a fictional New York town that apparently had only three employers: the hospital, organized crime, and the World Security Bureau—a global clandestine espionage agency that took down would-be supreme commanders of the world. As usual, something absurd was going on in that crazy soap opera—probably the underwear model-looking gangster was about to shoot someone or a patient was about to receive the first ever brain transplant—I don't even remember, but what I do remember is turning to Chris.

"I think I am going to be a doctor," I said.

He looked at me and laughed.

"Yeah right, braddah," he said. "You ain't no doctor."

He turned back to the show.

Everyone I've met since at medical school and hospitals and clinics, including my wife, knew that they were going to be doctors from the time they'd been five. Me, I didn't know the first thing about being a doctor, what it implied, or what a typical day for a doctor was even like. I didn't know the difference between Kimo and chemo. Hell, I didn't even know a doctor.

I just knew that Chris pissed me off.

I sat there and stewed.

I'd probably said "I think I am going to be a doctor" as a joke. Some young doctor on this soap opera was probably getting attention from a very attractive young nurse in the middle of an emergency. "Yes, Nurse Vining, I will accompany you back to your room for that extra exam, after I transplant this man's brain."

But for some reason it wasn't funny. I had been insulted many times by Chris, and I usually dished it back, but this time it was different. For whatever reason—maybe it was the hangover or the need to purge my stomach of all that food—I felt as if he had already made up his mind: that the closest I would ever get to being a doctor would be what we were doing right now, self-treating for the recovery from mild alcohol poisoning. It felt like a slap in the face. I knew he didn't mean anything that large-scale or personal, at the moment, but the message was clear: I was one of the boys, and the boys weren't doctor material.

The soap opera became unwatchable. The living room, with its empty beer bottles and crushed cigarette butts strewn across the carpet, suddenly stank. I began to see the entire student apartment complex, the place where I had wasted the last two-plus years, with its all-night kanilapila and *Street Fighter 2* gaming sessions, as a giant glue trap. All these years, all I wanted to do was be part of the group—in with the dark-haired and brown-skinned local braddahs who anesthetized their painful childhoods, both real and imagined, with drugs and alcohol. The ones who can be found outside every Hawaii high school even today, kicking back, looking cool, and wearing their Ainokea or All-in tee shirts. And I'd made it. I was one of them now. But as I sat there and thought how utterly stupid it was to be slouched on a couch watching a soap opera during a class that I was once again skipping, I wanted separation.

Was Chris trying to keep me down, crabs in a bucket? No, nothing like that. He was just being realistic. He was telling me, "No can."

I stood and shook his hand. "So what, party tonight?" he said.

"Yeah, man, I'll call you later."

It was a lie. I wasn't going to call. I wasn't going to return. As I walked down the stairs, heading for my car, which was sure to be tagged with my hundredth UH parking ticket, I was once again the child who had brought a lamp into an empty cardboard box and stared at the light. I was going to focus even if it blinded me.

....

A couple of days after being released from the ICU, I began to regain my senses. No more hallucinations, less and less fear. The giant needle stuck in my heart was removed, and I was told that I might be able to go home soon. Rualani and Lynn, of course, were right there with me. I could now whisper and was glad to be rid of the Sharpie and legal pad.

It was the day before my discharge that I realized none of my friends had been around during this ordeal. It didn't upset me or anything like that; I mean, it wasn't like I was in any condition to pick up the phone and say, "Hey, come to Hilo. I'm dying!" If I had, I'm sure a handful of friends would have flown over. But the fact that none of my friends were around, much less knew about what had happened, made me feel old.

Like any other kid, my friends were a huge part of my world growing up. In fact, like most dumb kids, there was a time when I would have chosen my "braddahs" over family. It wasn't until I was in college that I realized that friendship, while valuable, is proximity and common-interest based more than anything else. Binky, while my best friend growing up, was mostly so because we lived near each other and both got teased by the other neighborhood boys. Chris and Andy were my friends because we were all from Kahaluu, knew fishing and diving, went to the same high school, car pooled, and liked to party. My Hawaiian college buddies and I were close because we all dormed together and felt the camaraderie of being the first generation of Hawaiians from our little rural towns to be attending college.

Don't get me wrong—I love my friends and would do just about anything for them; however, it was my *family* at the hospital with me. It was my *wife* who held everything together when things got bleak. The bottom line: in the clinch, family trumps friends just about every time. The earlier kids learn this, the better off they'll probably be.

When my bloody, clot-filled catheter was finally removed, I was told that if I urinated, I could be discharged. It was Rualani who dragged me to the bathroom and held me up as I struggled to pee. I blasted out diarrhea instead. When I finally did pee, and began ripping IV's and EKG cords off me, the doctors told me that I could not go home without an oxygen tank, so it was Lynn who agreed to drive me to a medical supply warehouse and pick up what we needed while Rualani shot home to secure the oxygen compressor. I was wheeled out of the hospital connected to a tank with forty-five minutes of oxygen. Lynn raced to the warehouse. Forty-five minutes of air—it was like I was scuba diving through downtown Hilo.

When I finally got home and was connected to a fresh tank and enough hose to walk around the house twice, I asked Lynn to go to McDonald's drive-thru for me and pick a Quarter Pounder with Cheese, a large fries, a twenty-piece Chicken McNuggets, and a large chocolate shake. I was starving and apparently wanted my forty pounds back as soon as possible. She argued like hell, but finally did it.

For me, turning my back on my friends back in college was the first hard decision I'd ever made in my life. But almost twenty years later, as I sat in bed chowing down on thousands of calories of fried fast food, compliments of my wife, life once again confirmed it was the right decision.

Of course, it just might be that I was paying more attention to my Quaalude burger than my family. Just let me finish my McNuggets and pass out! Yes, those are doctor's orders: Let me slip back into a kanak attack coma.

As I drifted off, plastic tubes shooting oxygen up my nostrils, I thought how an Aloha Bowl from Hungry Lion tomorrow would hit the spot. I was regressing. But so many memories were crowding to the surface—The Boat, high school, the UH dorms, Marc and I not checking the mail, diving, and deciding to be a doctor while watching *General Hospital* when I was supposed to be in class. I really did watch my life flash, well, slo-mo, before my eyes. I thought about my old friends, most of whom I hadn't seen in years—work, marriage, parenthood, and family were now piloting most of our lives. But that wasn't really it, was it? The reason. No, I gave them up long before most of them got married, bought houses, and had kids.

Most people lose touch with old friends through relocation or parenthood. But my relationships did not simply fade with distance and time. Once I'd decided I was going to become a doctor, I'd consciously traded them in. Did I suspect that I'd one day pay a price for it? Hard to say. Maybe I repressed it. Anyway, here it was, back to haunt me with the question: was it worth it?

Chapter Four

Mau Imi Naauao (To Seek Continued Education)

Step one: I knew I had to temporarily ditch all my old friends and find new ones who would help me on my quest. Step two: all I knew was that doctors received excellent grades in school, so I set out to do good, whatever that meant. How hard could it be? I knew some nerds back in high school, and they didn't look that special.

How wrong I was.

For step one, all I did was hang out with the haoles in my science classes. I figured they must know doctors and know how to get good grades. I don't want to say my local friends weren't smart, but like criminal John would say, there were two kinds of smart. The first, book smart—I needed to become that kind of smart. The second, my "Kahaluu friends" smart—how not to get caught doing "stuff."—I already had covered, but that kind of smart wasn't helping me get A's in class. So I pulled off my local-Hawaiian superhero drinking suit, hung it in the closet, and jumped into my white freckled skin and looked for haoles to hang out with. I soon met someone who changed my life and became one of my best friends: Brian.

Brian was the perfect example of that guy you hear about, the one from middle-of-nowhere mainland, who left behind everything he had, joined the military, and eventually moved to Hawaii. In this case, Brian was from North Dakota.

He was a skinny white guy with dirty blonde hair, a crooked smile and birth control glasses (so called because they were so thick and ugly that there was no way he was going to get any action wearing them). He sat in the front row in organic chemistry class and, boy, did he know how to study. His military training had taught him discipline. The guy was a machine. Studying was a new discipline for me, but fortunately, after all those weekends on The Boat, I was no stranger to vomit-inducing hard work.

My plan was to clone what Brian did. I ate like him, slept like him and studied and studied and studied like him. No magic bullet, no gifted intelligence, just hard work. I had coasted through life up to this point, and my brain was not used to assimilating such massive quantities of information. But I figured it was like beer drinking: you just have to open wide and start pounding. It wasn't easy. Sometimes I would have to read the simplest things three or four times just to understand them. Then I'd have to read them again, dozens of times, in order to remember them. But as my Grandpa Schwartz used to say, "Your brain is a muscle. Work it out and it will get stronger," and mine did.

It was cold, robot-like work. Just like on The Boat with my dad, I simply followed orders, except this time, for the first time, they were my own. I didn't care how I felt, how long it took, or what was being barked at me. I plowed ahead, just like Brian. It was a little easier now that I was surrounded by people who I'd met in science classes and who lived and breathed school. They all were part of student government or in the Organic Chemistry Club, stuff like that, and I just slipped right in. Once in, I didn't hang back. I was never scared to work or to ask someone for help.

The whole time I knew I wouldn't fail. This may sound fairly arrogant, but remember, "no can" had never been uttered in my house growing up. Also, remember that with my mom and three sisters, asking for help was as natural as breathing for me. I was programmed for this.

So after wasting my first two-and-a half years of college partying, I officially broke most of my ties and studied my ass off. Instead of messing around in Hamillton Library with Marc and Chris, competing to find the biggest book in the place but never actually cracking its covers, I was actually going there to study.

Another person who helped me, besides Brian, was Kathy's boyfriend, Danny. He was about to graduate, so he was schooled in credit counting. We computed what I'd need to graduate with a B.A. in zoology. He figured that after three years of college, I only had one or two classes that would apply to my major. So it would take another four years to graduate. Looking back, he was wrong. It'd end up taking five.

Somehow, over the next five years, I went from a student on academic probation with 1.8 GPA to graduate with a 3.8 GPA. I received an A in every single class except one: evolutionary biology. I got a B+ in that one. I spent too much time trying to date the teacher's assistant. It's like Dad said, "Never shit where you eat."

Meanwhile, a few of my old friends, the minority who made it through college, moved on to grad school or started working "real jobs." Chris completed a master's degree in English and wrote a novel. Craig went to law school and became a public defender. Marc started off as a sports journalist, then jumped in P.R. And there I was, still living with my parents, still in school, making zero dollars. But I refused to get discouraged and did the work.

Perhaps the hardest baggage to shed over this half-decade study fest was my, and most of my old friends', "good enuff" philosophy. The phrase is local, but the sentiment is hardly unique to Hawaii. It's probably common every place where kids raised by poor or working class people are never able to forget the glass ceiling that hovers right over their heads. "No one with the last name 'Puana' will ever live in Kahala," my social studies teacher had said.

The "good enuff" philosophy goes something like this: I finished most of my homework. Good enuff. I chopped down half the banana trees in the backyard. Good enuff. I graduated from high school (barely) while my dad had not. Good enuff. I got a job working at a hotel and earn decent tips. Good enuff. I rent a two-bedroom, one bath apartment. Good enuff. My kid isn't starving and knows his ABCs. Good enuff. I don't gotta steal, sell ice, or go on welfare like my cousins. Good enuff.

If I wanted to become a doctor, good enuff was not going to cut it. My new science major friends didn't wreck their GPAs in their first two-and-a-half years of college. They were smarter, more ambitious, more driven than I'd ever been. Good enuff wasn't even in their lexicon. But all that wasn't the scary part. The scary part was that they were the competition. There are only so many med school slots per year, and we were all applying.

I couldn't just work as hard as my new peers. That was not good enuff. I had to work harder.

And I did. I studied so much that A's on exams weren't probable. They were guaranteed. I pressed my clunky short-term memory so hard that if my brain were really a muscle like my grandfather had said, it would've suffered lactic acid burn for five years straight. Eating was expendable, as was sleep.

Another adage that many of us local kids grew up hearing: don't be a panty. Well, I refused to be a panty; I studied my ass off. It was during these five years that I learned that embracing

the "good enuff" philosophy is, in fact, being a panty. Not finishing all your homework is being a panty. Not trying hard in
school is being a panty. Not teaching your kids more than just
the ABCs is being a panty.

"I'm too tired."

"I going have beers with my friends instead."

Panty-ass bitches.

I'm not saying that everything you teach your kids has to
be academic—on The Boat, my dad taught me vomit-inducing
hard work, which was a more lasting lesson than Shakespeare
or algebra. The main thing is, he spent the time teaching me.
Even though I slowed him down, even though I was probably
more of an irritant than a helpful first mate, leaving me at home
watching T.V. was not an option.

So I battled to fend off the good enuff philosophy that I'd
lived by for all my life. Instead, I embraced "don't be a panty."
And in total, it took me seven-and-a-half years to walk away
from the University of Hawaii with a bachelor's degree. It's
never too late to stop being a panty.

2.

During my last year of college, I spent my time prepping for
the upcoming hail-storm of medical school interviews. I would
interview at eight schools, including good ol' John A. Burns
School of Medicine at UH. I wanted to keep my options open,
but I had every intention of staying in Hawaii.

I was no stranger to the Mainland. During my undergraduate studies, with the help of a genetics professor, Rebecca Cann,

I had been admitted into a biomedical science program at Harvard University. Yeah, the red-headed Hawaiian actually went to Harvard for a little while.

Boston was strange, and people walked around talking really funny: Caaa (car), coinner(corner), Cawffee(Coffee). People there were nice, but as you can imagine, school was tough. I came from the University of Hawaii and Aloha and I entered Harvard University and Hell. No one helped each other and everything was a secret.

In class, I normally sat by the same guy. We were friendly up until I asked him an academic question for the first time. His face shifted from affable to disturbed.

"It wouldn't be fair to you or me if I helped you with this problem," he said.

I thought he was joking, so I started to laugh. He wasn't. He walked away and ignored me the rest of the day.

The next day in class, he started to talk to me like nothing had happened. At UH, we'd sit around a table and split a problem up. Here, everything was an individual competition filled with subterfuge. Also, the food sucked. For me, this was Harvard. This was the Mainland. And all I was thinking at the time was they could have it.

So I had escaped the Mainland as quickly as I could with the little piece of paper that said I completed a science program at Harvard.

When I got back to Hawaii, I studied for the entrance exam to medical school (the MCAT) for three months. I took the test, got my depressing results, and ran away from life. I was crushed.

Basically, going into the test I'd listened to some people—and when I say "people" I mean my neighbor, who was an English teacher, and my roommate's friend who was a massage therapist—who'd said I didn't have a shot of getting into med school unless I got a perfect score on the MCAT. They told me stories of geniuses who invented cancer-curing medicine and people who built state-of-the-art, hydro-powered hovercrafts who couldn't get in—wait, I think that hovercraft guy made it in, but only on the second try. I assumed that they were right and sat on my applications for awhile. I spent weeks pissed off and very tan from my now more frequent diving expeditions. I stopped going to class, and I probably wouldn't have completed my major if I continued down this road, but I finally showed my application to one of my friends at UH, Dr. Leslie Tam, who held a PhD in microbiology. He was the first person I talked to who was actually qualified to intelligently discuss my application.

I'd first met Dr. Tam while sitting in a courtyard, waiting for microbiology class to begin. A tanned Asian (which in Hawaii is about as common as fruit-bearing trees) wearing a dive watch sat next to me. I could tell he was older, but how much older I wasn't sure. It always seemed to me that most Asians looked as if they were in their mid-thirties up until about age seventy-five, when they suddenly appeared as if they were run over by the aging truck. Anyway, back then, I'd told this particular Asian that he had a nice watch and asked if it had a depth gauge on it. That was it. We started talking diving and fishing until class started. I was surprised that we entered the same classroom. I was further surprised when he stepped in front of the class, introduced himself as a substitute, and began to lecture.

After that day, we'd sometimes hang out. Sometimes we'd golf, and sometimes he'd even take me flying in his rickety twin-engine plane. The reason it took me so long to ask for his advice was because I was embarrassed to show him how I did on the MCAT. When I finally summed up the courage to meet him at his office, I prefaced the conversation by saying, "Do you think diesel mechanic school will take me?"

He smiled, browsed through the application, and handed it back to me. "I guess you'll be leaving Hawaii for some fancy school now," he said.

He explained that my application was excellent, my MCAT score was solid, and that I wouldn't have a problem getting into "somewhere." Somewhere? That word rang in my head. To me "somewhere" meant the Antarctic. And there was no way I was moving from Hawaii again. I'd had my fill of the Mainland in Boston. I knew Dr. Tam had a lot of pull at the University of Hawaii's John Burns School of Medicine, so I acted calm and cool and said, "Thanks. You know I am not leaving Hawaii."

The words of many a stubborn local boy. Only offer us tourism jobs that are either tip-based or middle-management? I don't care. I'm not leaving. Jack up home prices to the point where Hawaii is the second-most expensive place to buy land per square foot in the nation? I don't care. I'm not going. Flood the islands with a bunch of Steves, haoles who feed the tourism industry, then decide to move here, and are the reason why property prices skyrocket in the first place? Screw you, buddy, I'm not going anywhere.

I know local people who aren't into nature or Hawaiiana, hardly ever leave their air-conditioned Americana suburban homes except to go to work or golf, and never go to the beach, and they still refuse to leave this place.

It's like the by-now tired squid eye analogy. When you dive, you either can spot a squid hole, or you can't. There's no teaching it. Either you recognize this place as the best place to reside in the world, or you don't. You can't teach it. You can't teach love.

And I was in love more than most. Like others, most of my friends and family were here. On top of that, I loved the ocean. By now, I'd seen beaches on the Mainland. What a joke. I was also a chameleon here. If I wanted to hang out with my local friends, as the red-headed Hawaiian, I could slip right in. If I wanted to hang out with my haole science group, no problem. I could pass. I had options. As far as I knew, in the Mainland, that option would be reduced to one.

Finally, I was Hawaiian by blood. This was my home, dammit. How could someone tell me that I had to go live somewhere else?

But I heeded Leslie's advice and applied to a bunch of schools. I'd come perilously close to being a panty before he snapped me out of it. So I flew to the Mainland and interviewed for every single program that I'd applied to. I smiled through every question. I promised to bring a ray of tropical sunshine to all their hospitals. I was the red-headed Hawaiian—after years of teasing and verbal battles, no one could fluster me. And I was accepted by just about every place. Tulane, Washington, Creighton, New York. Creighton's medical school offered me a two-hundred thousand dollar Dean's scholarship. New York Medical University offered to pay half my tuition.

Hawaii's John A. Burns School of Medicine put me on their waiting list. Wait, are you kidding?

The waiting list. I was being wooed by several power-house medical schools and was accepted at every other school I interviewed for and Hawaii put me on the what? There were only about a dozen or so full-ride med school academic scholarships available in the entire nation, and I was offered one of them. And Uncle John puts me on the waiting list.

Obviously, still a sore spot for me. Hawaiian blood with all the qualifications: stellar GPA, solid entrance exam scores, research at Harvard, and volunteer work: Denied.

Albeit, I was only on that wait-list a week before they sent me my acceptance letter.

But I was pissed.

When I opened my UH med school acceptance letter, I was in the car with my mom. "What does it say?" Mom asked.

"UH accepted me."

Mom frowned. "But what about the other schools?"

She wanted me to get out of Hawaii. She thought if under-grad took me over seven years to complete at UH, getting out of UH medical school would probably take me another forty. She figured here, I'd always be on Hawaiian time.

I skimmed the letter again then casually ripped it up. "I'm going to Creighton," I said. "I'm part pake too, after all."

Mom smiled.

It was a no-brainer. In 1999, I chose the full scholarship at Creighton. I was headed to Nebraska. But to this day, I'm not sure whether I made the decision more so because of money or because the John Burns School of Medicine had hurt my feelings.

3.

Nebraska is pretty much smack dab in the middle of the conti-nental United States. Any image you conjure up in your head, even if you haven't been there, is probably accurate. Yes, there's a lot of corn. Yes, there's seemingly an endless supply of dry, flat land that extends to the horizon. Yes, there's seasons and snow. And yes, there are a ton of white people, over ninety-three percent of the state's population, last I heard.

God, the seasons. In Hawaii, seasons are simple. The waves get big on the south shore in the summer, and they get big on the north shore in the winter. Typical Hawaii weather report no matter what month it is: partly cloudy with highs near the 80's. The report—thirty seconds max.

Nebraska was a completely different story. The TV news weather report was as exciting as a pay-per-view fight night. There would be the *ultra sensitive forecast 4000 Doppler radar* on one channel and *the max-weather alert system 8000* on another channel. To me it seemed insane—weather forecasting, projection models, NASA satellite images, and weathercams. The *National Center of Erratic Weather* was stationed just down the road at Strategic Air Command (SAC) Air Force Base. Weather would often be the lead news story. Prime time television would be interrupted by emergency weather reports:

"Freak blizzard hits 34th and Main!"

"Freak hailstorm approaches! Put your car in the garage now!"

Just keeping apprised of this stuff could turn into a full-time job.

I never really got into weather reports, which was pretty stupid for someone living in Nebraska. I would go to class in slippers and a tank top, and five hours later, it would be snowing. Once, I was walking to my car in an ice storm wearing slippers and a tee shirt and a guy stopped me and asked if I was cold. I could barely hear him over the Eskimo baby seal parka that partially covered his mouth.

"You think this is cold, you should see where I'm from," I said.

"Where?" he asked.

"Hawaii." I walked away, leaving him there, mouth agape.

I was cruising around with a bad attitude. I could have been attending med school in Hawaii if it weren't for my stupid pride.

Then there was daylight savings time. Who the hell invented this? To me, it was like saying, "Today feels like a Friday, so let's change the day of the week." All I knew was that twice a year, I had to go around and change every clock in the house. I had to bust out the car manual to change the clock radio, usually while I was driving. After a few years, I decided not to change it. Of course, I started to get confused and arrived late to places, so within a couple of weeks, I realized my rebellion was not going to last and finally had to conform.

Anyway, when I first arrived in Nebraska, Rualani was there to meet me at the airport to help me get situated (yes, once again, an older sister to the rescue). She helped move my stuff into a one-bedroom, one-bath student apartment that sat atop the Jayhawk Bar. She made sure I had everything I'd need, stuff I'd forget about if left to my own devices, like soap, toothpaste, and breathing.

One of the first formal functions I attended was the short white coat ceremony and Ru came with me. Each student (there were about a hundred-and-five of us in the class) received a short white coat as we began our journey into medicine.

It was here that I met two other beginning med students from Hawaii. From them, I discovered there were so many folks from Hawaii that, in fact, they had a Hawaiian club and a yearly

Me, five years old at the beach.

Me at age one-and-a-half at my house after dad went fishing and then bottom-fishing on Molokai.

Dashingly handsome picture at school. Fourth grade.

Boat, 1982.

7-6-84

Mom cutting bait when I was twelve.

Dad with mahimahi when
I was two years old.

Dad with ahi when I was not even born yet.
That's why he looks so angry.

The Kathy.

Me in my
baseball gear,
kicking ass and
taking names at
age eight.

My sister, Kathy, and I.

Me at my St. Ann's May Day celebration, about thirteen years
old.

I'm on the ugly couch at age twelve.

Freshman year,
high school.

Football practice.

Me at UH college graduation.

Mom and Dad in 2005.

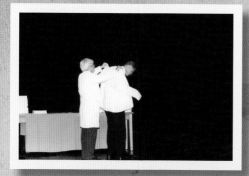

Me at my white coat ceremony getting my first doctor's coat. It's a short coat. You don't get a long one until you're a doctor after medical school graduation.

Lynn and I as interns at Scott and White hospital.

Me as a medical student.

Lynn and I as third year medical students in our engagement picture.

Happy Holidays 2001

On our very first
Christmas The Puana
Farm wishes you love
peace and happiness..
Lynn, Rudy, Simba
Apollo, Tex, Tom, Jerry
Doe, Duke, Curly and

Lynn and I on our first farm in Omaha with our ducks, horses, and dogs.

Lynn and I on a cruise in the Bahamas.

luau. I was relieved. Ru probably was, too, and headed back home.

However, over the course of that first year, I found myself unsettled by my fellow students from Hawaii.

It wasn't that the vast majority of these students were Asian. But an awful lot of them were like the Sams who named themselves Kamuela, the Davids who named themselves Kawika, and the Steves who wore koa fishhooks around their necks back home. Even here, in the middle-of-nowhere Nebraska, it was cool to be Hawaiian. So these Asian students were actually calling themselves Hawaiian because no one knew the difference.

This part did not bother me. In a way, it was flattering. They'd abandoned their own heritage and wanted to be Hawaiian. Cool. However, whenever I was around, they felt guilty for calling themselves Hawaiian, so they would go out of their way to explain the difference between being born and raised in Hawaii and being Native. Inevitably, when they'd explain this, to say, a cute blond co-ed, she would ask, "Oh. So who is the native one?"

They'd point to me. Red-headed and freckled.

And then another cute girl would say, "That cute guy Lance in your class is like a tribal Hawaiian guy, do you know him?"

Right, the world renowned Hawaiian kahuna and tribal leader Dr. Lance Taniguchi. It was hilarious.

Poor guys. My very presence was a cock block. Soon they got tired of having to explain. And I started feeling guilty that they felt that they had to. I got it. It sounded way cooler to the girls to say their genes emerged from the primordial soup of tribal life and Aloha Spirit than it was to say their Asian ancestors were shipped over to Hawaii like cattle to pick sugar cane in indentured servitude for some haole rich guy because all the natives were dying.

So I started to drift away from the local Hawaii crowd and started hanging out with the haoles. This, of course, came with its own set of problems. Some of them would say that they could see the Asian in me after they heard the last name "Puana." Most of them thought Hawaiians were Asians. Others, upon hearing that the Native population in Hawaii made up less than ten percent of the state's population, would ask, "How is that possible? I have been to Hawaii and there were natives all over the place." Now, without the Lance Taniguchis around, it was up to me to explain. I stopped trying after about a month.

At least I didn't have to. Once again, the red hair, source of my childhood sorrow, was paying dividends. If I didn't say anything, they all assumed I was haole anyway. They left me alone to study. After all, med school was as hard as advertised.

............4.

It was during my first year that I met and got to know Lynn Marie Welch. We were in anatomy class together. The students were separated by tables, and I was stuck with what had to be the three most competitive, shrill, and petty women in med school:

"It's my turn to cut!"

"No, it's my turn to cut!"

"No, the arm is mine!"

"It's my eyeball!"

As this was getting old fast, I looked over at the next table, where Lynn and a few other students seemed to be getting along splendidly. The semester progressed, and I found myself drifting to that table. There were perks besides them being overall nice, fun people. One plus for me was the first time the students were introduced to surgical scrubs. Lynn, who was very attractive, had trouble with hers. Instead of wearing the specially designed scrubs for women, which had a high v-neck that prevented drooping, she unknowingly wore standard male scrubs. Basically, it was cleavage city. I still remember one particular bra she wore—a jeweled, purple flower in the middle of intersecting straps.

I had noticed Lynn early on; in fact, when Rualani had first spotted her at the short white coat ceremony, she'd told me: "One day, you're going to marry that girl."

So there I was, trying to hook up in a room full of dead bodies. I'd go up to her while she'd be cutting into a cadaver and say stuff like, "What's a girl like you doing in a place like this?"

I learned that she had grown up in Nebraska, attended Michigan, and had been a Wolverine cheerleader. I told her about Hawaii. To her, I was like the barbarian of our class. I was the only one who wore tank-tops and had tattoos. I'd go to school in rubber slippers. "Are you the one who got the Dean's Scholarship?" she once asked.

"Yeah," I said. I was the one who'd won the full-ride scholarship, that many, like her, had applied for.

Then she asked, "Why are you like thirty then?"

Ouch.

My first Halloween in Nebraska I went to the med school party dressed as a man in wind. My hair was gelled back, a wire hanger suspended my necktie up in the air, and rods placed in my sleeves and leggings created the visual effect of a man walking through a storm. Lynn was there dressed as a Spice Girl. We were all drinking, and I made up some excuse to get her in the kitchen alone with me. She followed.

Then I just mauled her.

I know, romantic. But it seemed to work. We've been together ever since. Why was she into me? I could make her laugh, which was, of course, huge. But why did she look past (or directly at?) the drinking, tank-tops, rubber slippers, and tattoos?

She thought: I can change him.

Luckily, her father was fine with what he saw as his daughter's attempt at genetic variation. I wasn't a big, black Hawaiian three-hundred-pounder, after all. I was the red-headed Hawaiian who looked haole. And now, unlike during my father's era, it was cool to be Hawaiian, even in Nebraska.

5.

Winters in Nebraska were brutal, cold, unpredictable, and lonely. Fortunately, I was lucky enough to spend my first Thanksgiving in Nebraska meeting and eating dinner with my future wife's family. Real cooking and watching Mainland folks in their homes? It would be like going on anthropological field work. I couldn't wait.

Early on in my life on the Mainland, I'd picked up hints that Hawaii customs were not standard across America. In most homes across the Mainland, dinner was a formal event that revolved around real conversations. Lynn's family was no different. It was obvious by their comfortable mannerisms that eating at the same table was a normal ritual. When I told them that we really didn't eat dinner together back home, that we all got our dinner trays and scrambled in front of the TV or on the patio, they looked at me like I had a third eye. Even basic family structures and interactions were different on the Mainland; not bad, different.

In Hawaii, kids lived with their parents indefinitely because most young people could not afford anything habitable. Even at thirty years of age, it was common for people in Hawaii to be sleeping in the same bedroom just as they did in high school. The best thing they could hope for in adulthood was a newly installed side door, so they could go in and out as they pleased. Both kids and parents knew that there was a good chance that they'd be living together for ages, so family members used dinner time to take a break from each other.

In the Mainland, eighteen-years-old and you're out. Mainlanders value their family time at the dinner table because they knew it was temporary, fleeting. It had an expiration date. Best make good use of it.

Anyway, I avoided making ass, and from that first Thanksgiving dinner on, Lynn's parents and I got along well. It didn't hurt that her parents were not strangers to Hawaii. They had a condo there and loved the islands. Her father, Gordon, was a well-read man who liked to work with his hands, and he was one of the only Mainlanders I'd met who knew what a Native Hawaiian was: "You don't look Samoan," he said.

Close enough.

Even better was the fact that Gordon was a pilot. I'd actually learned to fly back home during college (before I learned, I'd told my friend Chad that I wanted to fly. He laughed at me.

Five months later, I was cruising the sky). So Gordon and I always had a lot to talk about. My potential son-in-law resume looked pretty good as well: soon-to-be-doctor; Hawaiian, but haole-looking; pilot; and I treated Lynn with the love and respect she deserved.

And, I didn't hug them. Lynn always had to remind me that some people in the Mainland did not hug to greet each other or say goodbye. What she really meant was *her* people.

In Hawaii, I'd grown up hugging everyone, as did everyone else I knew. In the Mainland, you hug a girl and she screams, "Patriarchal oppressor!" Hug a guy—no way. Hug a child, super-bad move, they think you're a sexual deviant. Still I'd often forget myself and open wide with the arms. Then Lynn would have to jump in and say, "Sorry, he's from Hawaii. They all do that there."

It sometimes felt as if I was her mentally deficient child, ramming his helmeted head against a wall, and she had to explain my condition.

But I did not hug Lynn's parents at Thanksgiving, and fortunately, I did not call them "aunty" or "uncle" as well. I even wore my shoes in the house. Another interview passed with flying colors.

6.

Despite the fact that I was fortunate enough to have received a full scholarship to Creighton, money problems surfaced during that first year.

My small apartment, which was rent-free, was furnished with two things: my stereo and my futon. I couldn't afford a new wardrobe, which explained the tank tops, shorts and slippers. What little money I had was being spent on eggs.

Why eggs? When I'd first arrived in Nebraska, I went shopping and there they were, ninety-nine cents a dozen. I couldn't believe it, and I took advantage. With no income coming in, I ate eggs. Lots and lots of eggs. Dozens and dozens. I ate them until just the look of them made me gag.

There was a time, during that first year, when for the first time in my life I felt poor, and I learned that being poor can make one angry. There I was, a Hawaiian, busting my ass in med school. Wasn't I entitled to some help? I resented the fact that the multi-billion-dollar Kamehameha Schools trust, an institution for Native Hawaiians, wasn't knocking on my door to tell me I'd won the sweepstakes.

I was sulky for awhile. A diet of eggs can do that to a man. But my father would have slapped me across the head if he'd known what was going through it.

I think I was simply missing Hawaii, missing my family and friends. I was sacrificing them so that I could freeze my ass off in Nebraska. For my friends, life was moving along, but I would not be there to witness the landmark moments. I was asked to be best man at one of my friend's weddings and a groomsman in four others. I made it to one. I heard stories about my friend Dean, a fellow Native Hawaiian, who, newly married, returned to Hawaii after medical school and had to move back in with his parents until he could pay off his student loans. He was a doctor, and he had to move in with his parents? Are you kidding me?

I decided to apply for a Kamehameha Schools grant to help with living expenses. The process drove me even more crazy. A mountain of bureaucratic paperwork and proposals that took so long to fill out, they hurt me academically because I was studying about one-hundred-and-twenty hours a week. On top of the forms, I was required to do a community service project to help my fellow, less fortunate Hawaiians. Again my anger got the best of me. Wouldn't it be smarter to support me until I could get to a position where I could better help the Hawaiian people rather than requiring it of a person barely treading water himself? I mean, you're going to force me to be socially responsible—will I want to do it again when given the choice? I was outraged.

If it wasn't for my sister Kathy's help, I wouldn't have completed the application. Kathy, who blazed through an undergraduate degree, a master's degree, and a law degree in seven years after barely graduating from high school. Her words of wisdom: "Rudy, just shut up and stop complaining. It'll be good for you. Give me the paperwork."

So after that first year of med school, with Kathy's help, I left Lynn behind and returned to Hawaii during the summer. I volunteered at Waianae Community Hospital only so that Kamehameha Schools would give me money. My attitude was still sour.

The Waianae property was more clinic than hospital, a small oasis of health care for people who had no other place to go. The majority of the patients were Hawaiian, homeless, with zero access to primary health care. Patients came to the emergency room to receive care for pregnancy, drug overdose, even sunburn. Hypertension and diabetes was endemic. Having diabetes and being Hawaiian was like being Chinese and Hawaiian: If you were Hawaiian, you probably had both.

I was volunteering on the side of the island hidden away from tourists. I helped out as much as I could. As a first year medical student, I was just trying to make sure I didn't hurt any patients. Bob and Milo, the two who ran the place, let me sleep in the back office when I was trying to rack up as many community hours as possible in the shortest amount time. Mother Theresa I wasn't, and they didn't ask me to be her.

I finished the summer and flew back to the wasteland I now called home.

On the flight back home, I had a lot on my mind. It was hard for me to return to the Mainland. I wanted to stay home. However, I wasn't a quitter. The only thing I'd ever quit was the Cub Scouts, and that was because the blue suit and yellow scarf clashed terribly with the red hair—I'd looked like the personification of the Romanian flag.

Anyway, before the plane even left the tarmac, the blue-haired pudge sitting next to me claimed the middle arm rest. She sat with her legs open. Each time I relaxed, our knees touched. And when they did, hers remained immovable. She asked me where I was from. "Hawaii," I said. She asked what branch of the military my father was in. I explained. The entire time I was talking, I could sense that she was waiting for a lull—enough about you, let's talk about me.

The lull came, and I got her story, from cradle to retirement. Then the topic turned to Hawaii:

"This was my tenth trip to Hawaii, and I was thinking of living there, but I am always too happy to go home. I just get island fever too bad, and I would miss the seasons too much."

Island fever: I'd heard this phrase many times before.

Island fever: if my home makes you ill, maybe you shouldn't visit.

By the time the plane reached the Mainland, I couldn't wait to get off. Yet, oddly, I felt revitalized and enthusiastic. While the

woman on the plane had been droning on and on, I was thinking about the community work I'd done in Waianae and began
to realize was that Kamehameha Schools was right to put me
through that experience. I'd been mad at first because I misun-
derstood the school's intent. I thought they were making me
jump through these hoops to force me to be socially responsible.
What I finally realized was that they were showing me who it
was that truly needed help. It was crazy that I expected to be
coddled when there were Hawaiians out there suffering expo-
nentially more than me. This realization gave me a new-found
direction and enthusiasm, and a real desire to help Hawaiians.

7.

In the middle of my second year of medical school, Lynn and
I were talking one day. From her, I learned a startling fact: Students had to complete this thing called a residency after med
school to become doctors.

Wait, what? I thought med school was just four years, then,
boom, you're a doctor.

Nope, residency is four more years, five for some.

In typical Rudy fashion, I'd started something I knew very
little about. Like my dad building his very first boat—if I were
so lucky. After learning more about this residency business, it
dawned on me that I might not live in Hawaii until I was forty,
if ever.

I was twenty-nine-years old. I had two more years of med
school and at least four years of residency to complete. I was in

a serious relationship with a woman from Nebraska who loved horses and wide-open spaces, a woman who had zero desire to move to Hawaii.

She also explained some other factors that showed why moving to Hawaii made little sense. All the prestigious residency programs were on the Mainland. Hawaii's cost of living was too high. She wanted acres and horses, and both would cost a fortune on the islands. And then there was the pay—compared to doctors on the Mainland, doctors in Hawaii made little money. On top of that, unlike me and my tuition ride, Lynn was borrowing to cover her education. She would owe about a quarter million dollars in student loans after all was said and done.

What could I say? She was right on all accounts. And I loved her. I had to start getting used to the idea that I might end up living on the mainland for the rest of my life. The more I accepted it, the more bleak my prospects seemed. It was like going out on the boat with Dad: nothing to look forward to but blood and fish guts and puke.

Still, my second year of med school was relatively uneventful. I moved out of my one-bedroom student apartment. A friend agreed to not charge me rent if I renovated his basement (some of Dad's hard teaching, paying off again.) While not banging away with a hammer, I studied like hell. Lynn and I started talking future more and more. She refused to move in with me until we were married. In fact, she also refused to participate in a couples match (a program in which couples can apply to the same residency programs together so that they are not split up) until we were married. Apparently, she really wanted to marry me.

And still I missed home. Lynn would ask me what I missed about it the most. Let's see—the people, the beaches, the weather, friends, family, diving, scenery, *Hawaiian Fishing News*; I could have gone on and on, but all I usually said was, "The food." I think she knew it was more than that.

By year three, med school curriculum switched from classroom-based to hospital-based; it was time to decide on a residency specialization and shop for an engagement ring.

Getting to pick a specialization was the only bright spot we had as third-year med students. Most of our time was spent being abused in hospitals. The residents hated us because we slowed them down with our stupid questions. The staff physicians hated us because they felt as if they had to hold our hands or we'd do something stupid and they'd be sued. The nurses didn't hate us, but it would be the last chance they'd get to boss us around, so they took full advantage. And of course, the patients wanted nothing to do with us. Who wants a student working on them? Overall, we were liabilities. We got coffee a lot. Those short white coats we had been so proud to receive before we started our first year of med school? We were now embarrassed to wear them. The coats were just constant reminders to everyone, including ourselves, that we weren't real doctors.

But at least we got to choose what type of doctor we would eventually become. Most already knew. They wanted to be orthopedic surgeons, pediatricians, or cardiologists all of their lives. Despite her stellar grades and reputation, Lynn wanted to specialize in internal medicine. She wanted to become a flea. We called internists fleas because they were the last ones to jump off a dying dog (in other words, the last doctor patients would see before they died) and, of course, there were so many of them.

As for me, I flip-flopped constantly before settling on anesthesiology. To me, anesthesiologists had this cool, like Samoan strip-club bouncers back home. Arms crossed, looking disinterested, as if they'd seen and done it all before. They also made good money while standing around looking cool. The job was ninety-nine percent boredom and one percent sheer terror.

With my specialization finally decided on, it was time for me to tackle my other big third-year project: getting Lynn to marry me.

The problem, of course, was the ring. Apparently I was supposed to spend two months' salary on this thing, but had never come across one that cost zero dollars. Back then, I didn't know anything about stocks, but I was desperate to make some quick cash. After a friend's prompting, I stuck what little money I had into a company called eConnect. My money tripled in a week. More friends joined in. Within a month, we were so far up, all of us med student amateur investors decided to take a road trip to Kansas City. It was a Thursday and unfortunately my classmate Joe and I had to stay behind. Joe had a project due at the hospital on Saturday, and I had to ask Lynn to marry me.

So, Joe and I were home on Friday morning and I was sick to my stomach. I had to take all my money out of eConnect, so I could make the payment on Lynn's engagement ring, due that Saturday. I decided that if I was going to take all my money out of the fastest rising stock of the new century, I needed to convince Joe to do the same. Misery loves company and all that jazz.

My efforts started at breakfast:

"Joe could you pass the milk, oh and by the way, get out now!"

He ignored me.

But after he finished his Lucky Charms, we both sold that Friday.

On Saturday, our friends returned from Kansas City and said that there was rumor of a huge eConnect announcement planned for Monday. They were giddy. Some speculated that maybe Microsoft was going to buy the company. Sick to my stomach, I went to the jewelry store and paid for Lynn's engagement ring.

Monday morning came, and we were all crowded around the computer. I was quasi happy for my gloating friends. They were about to make a fortune. They teased and said they would buy me a Porsche when it was all over. Joe was fuming. He even decided to buy more stock right when the market opened.

Joe tried to put in his order. He kept refreshing it, over and over again, but the order would not be received.

"Crap!" Joe said. "The stock must be going through the roof! They won't even take my order!"

While the high fives filled the room, Joe kept refreshing his order. Then a single news update appeared at the bottom of the computer screen:

"SEC Halts E-Connect trading for false statements and illegal activity." Joe casually clicked the cancel order button, got out of his chair, and hugged me. Besides Lynn, I believe he was the first person to hug me on the Mainland. The stock reopened a few months later at a penny a share.

8.

The summer after our third year, Lynn and I were to be married in Hawaii at the Royal Hawaiian Hotel. I knew my brother-in-law Doug (Rualani's husband) was going to be the best man. After all, he'd taught me to drive and smoke a joint when I was a kid. Binky, Joby, Chris, and Andy were in my wedding party as well. I invited a couple of my Mainland friends to the wedding, too. My only regret was almost not including Todd, my old friend who I went to school with longer than anyone else.

As mentioned in a previous chapter, Todd and I went to elementary school and high school together. He was our class president at Mid-Pac and received a full-ride football scholarship our senior year. He was smart, confident, and charismatic, but as we all graduated high school, and our lives took different trajectories.

Todd knocked up his girlfriend, didn't go to college, and entered the work force upon graduation. Whenever I'd make it back home, I'd selfishly not visit him because it hurt to see his potential gone to waste. The guy could've done anything with his life. He could've been in med school with me.

Before the wedding, when my wife was sending out invitations, she said she couldn't find Todd's address. I told her I'd find it later. He almost didn't get invited and barely made it to the wedding. When I saw him, I knew I had made a huge mistake. I'd even starting telling myself that he would have just gotten into a fight with my friends from the Mainland even though I knew that wasn't true. What was wrong with me? I was turning more haole than most haoles. And I was supposed to be the Hawaiian.

I'm using the term haole not as shorthand for race, but for an attitude. All haole meant was thinking of yourself before others. And I was doing just that with my shabby treatment of Todd. He should've been in my wedding party, but because he wasn't living up to *my* expectations, he almost didn't even get invited. Med school, the Mainland, my self-involvement, were turning me into someone I was not liking very much.

Joby, one of my groomsmen, who I also went to high school with, was the perfect example of what I meant by haole not being race-based. He was full Caucasian, and if he'd grown up in Kahaluu like me, he would have been treated badly just because of the color of his skin. Add to that the granola, wilderness look of him, and it would have been even worse. But Joby was never haole. Of all my friends, he alone knew how much I missed the water, and he'd drop whatever he was doing and made it a point to make sure that during each infrequent trip home, I'd make it to the ocean.

The day before the wedding, it was no different. There was no crazy bachelor party with booze and strippers, just an all-day diving trip. Joby, Doug, my nephew Douglas (Doug and Rualani's son), and I loaded up our scuba gear and headed out to Makapuu. I got a big shock when my father, who had not been diving since his second trip to the decompression chamber, joined us. It had been over three decades since the old man put on his fins.

Joby was the best natural diver I'd ever met. He'd been the one who introduced me to diving for mahi mahi, ono, and ulua at depths as low as two-hundred feet. His lungs were so big and efficient that when he'd go under, he'd leave a trail of tiny air bubbles that resembled rabbit turds. Often, when my tank would be running low, we'd switch because his would still be nearly full. Haole? I don't think so. Ever the conservationist, he'd also measure and catalog his catch of fish and lobster.

Again, to me haole means selfishness, but the definition is mine, and others carry different meanings of the word. To some, haole means person from Mainland who doesn't know what the hell he or she is doing. In that regard, my brother-in-law and part-Hawaiian nephew were the haoles that day; only a half-mile off the coast, and poor Doug got seasick. Douglas, who normally held up pretty well on boats, got sick as well. Neither caught anything.

Then there was my dad. While Joby, Doug, Douglas and I armed ourselves with state-of-the-art gauges, electronics, and spear guns—which is kind of the haole approach to diving—my father just grabbed an old tank, a kui, and a three-pronged Hawaiian sling. At least his tank had a pressure gauge on it, although he didn't even know what that was. Dad looked as anxious as I felt. He was once again the boy who'd wanted to impress his father, the boy who needed to catch enough to feed a family of fourteen. Me, I was anxious about Dad coming to harm on the day before my wedding.

Well, guess who was the first in the water and the last one up. When he did finally surface, his tank was bone dry and his stringer was full. We looked on, amazed. "I dive till it gets hard to breathe," he said.

Joby and I could always catch fish but not like this. For this kind of assault, someone would have to be thinking of the next fish before taking down the current one. Also, when he speared a fish, there was no fist pumping or showing off. For Dad, it was all business. Like I've said, the man was nails.

The bachelor party was perfect. I had my best man, my nephew, one of my best friends, and my father out in the ocean with me. The wedding itself went splendidly—Todd made it, and mostly due to Rualani's tireless coordination, rounding up bridesmaids and groomsmen like cattle for fittings, rehearsals, and picture-taking, the ceremony went down without a hitch. When Ru was shouting instructions to us on my wedding day,

Chris leaned over to me. "Wow, she's just like your mom," he said.

I nodded. We Puana men have been blessed with the strength, generosity, and industrious nature of the Puana women. Now another woman was being added to the mix, an ex-Michigan cheerleader from Nebraska. Lynn Marie Welch Puana would fit right in.

9.

Lynn and I returned to Nebraska as husband and wife for our fourth and last year of medical school. After I spent a few weeks sulking, missing home, Lynn showed me a listing for a house for sale in Nebraska. It was fifty grand. She then showed me a listing for a similar-looking house in Hawaii. It went for over half a million. We took out a loan and bought the Nebraska house. Dad flew up and helped us renovate. Loans were easy to get for soon-to-be doctors, so we soon flipped the house and upgraded to another that sat on four acres. At last Lynn got her horses, and I was became resigned to a life outside of Hawaii.

As we applied to residency programs, I only had one stipulation: nowhere cold. During our last year in medical school, still stubbornly ignoring weather reports, I was wearing tee-shirt and slippers when my car died between twenty-foot-high walls of plowed snow. I thought this would be the end of me. Afterwards I told Lynn that we were not doing our residencies north of the Mason-Dixon Line.

She agreed. Well, kind of. We applied to fourteen programs in the South and two in the North (of course Hawaii did not have a program in my chosen field). Just in case, she said.

Domestic life was interesting. It was during our stay at our first house that I started noticing the similarities between Lynn and my mother. She did all of the cooking but wasn't the best of cooks (sorry, Mom). She was a whirlwind of energy who was in complete control of the household and our schedules. And one day, just like my dad, I found myself on allowance.

She was a star medical student and wanted to be an internist, so just about every hospital wanted her. It was rare to get a student of her caliber specializing in internal medicine (hence the influx of foreign-born primary care physicians these days—residency programs must meet demand); I just rode on her coattails. Now that we were married, we applied as a couple. You want her, you have to take me, too. This was important because my specialty, anesthesiology, was a competitive field. Anesthesiologists were the cool guys who liked their jobs—the hours were sane, and the pay was fabulous. Let the other guys work 24/7, always on call and never catching any sleep.

Doctors were only now catching on. Not long after I applied, applications to anesthesiology programs would triple.

Lynn and I drove cross-country to check out the hospitals we were applying to. We hit the Texas schools first. The long drive was torturous for both me and my wife. It was the first time I'd driven this distance, and my God, the scenery looked the same mile after mile. Lynn had to listen to me say "are we there yet?" for days. It got so bad, she refused to let me look at a map. When we hit the Texas border, I celebrated. Lynn just shook her head. It would take two more days to hit Galveston.

One of the hospitals we looked at in Texas was Scott and White Hospital, which was located in Temple and run by Texas

A&M University. Temple was a dump in the middle of nowhere. The monstrosity of a hospital was the sole employer. Other than that, there was a one-story strip mall and a movie theater that showed ninety-nine-cent matinees. The parking lots accommodated travel trailers for families on the go (because who in their right minds would stay here permanently). The fanciest restaurant was Chili's. Lynn and I agreed that we would not spend the next four years of our lives here.

However, upon investigating further, we found out that this hospital had fantastic facilities and world-class training second-to-none. It had a one-hundred percent anesthesia board pass rate, and its graduates were in the top one percent, salary-wise, in the nation. I started to see dollar signs, so instead of picking the other hospitals with more cosmopolitan settings, we eventually decided to live in wife-beater central in the middle of vast nothingness.

It would be in Temple that I'd first hear the phrase: If I owned both Texas and Hell, I would rent out Texas and live in Hell.

So we returned to Nebraska set on doing our residencies in Temple. My father-in-law and I had bought a small plane that cost less than a used car. I'd occasionally fly from the Midwest to Texas to scout my soon-to-be home. The vast tracts of never-ending dry land were sectioned off in squares. The ocean in the Gulf of Mexico was an expanse of gray, the water hazy with brownish foam cresting at the top of incoming waves. There were thin, scattered piles of trash along the high water mark, full of plastic jugs, packaging and used band-aids. These piles oozed a film of motor oil that coated the surface of the ocean.

Even the beaches were covered with a fine, gray silt and ubiquitous brown foam. Estuaries with sickly-looking mangrove trees scattered the shoreline. Their gnarled roots snared plastic bags and trapped more brown foam. Seagulls hung onto the mangroves, heads crooked like vultures. The birds, which were supposed to be pure white, were dirty, scrawny, and wore permanent stains the color of the brown foam.

I was basically moving to the Bizarro Hawaii. Hawaii after the apocalypse. In Hawaii, every few miles or so, you enter an area with its own history and place name. Just driving north from my home in Kahaluu, you'd pass Waiahole, Waikane, Kualoa, and Kaawa in twenty minutes. In Texas, a twenty-minute drive would not even get you one percent of the way from one nameless place to another. In Hawaii, we had mangroves, too. However, ours hid delicious haole, Hawaiian, blue-pincher, and Samoan crabs. Ours were fronted by fat mullet that we'd spear while torching at night. In Texas, if you went torching you would probably set the ocean on fire. Or if you were lucky, you'd spear the occasional rubber tire or an empty tube of Mexican toothpaste.

Lynn and I finished medical school, and as was tradition, joined the other soon-to-be doctors in our burning of the short white coat ceremony. Four years ago, we were so proud to receive these coats. Now, at the end of med school, we just wanted to see them reduced to ashes.

After the ceremony, Lynn and I began packing. We were moving from one wasteland to another. This was becoming a pattern that I was not enjoying, but if it made financial sense I felt there was no other choice.

After coming home from the hospital post near death experience, I spent a month in the house on oxygen, mostly watching TV. I was too weak to do much else. Upstairs, on my computer, sat a draft of this book you're reading now. I'd started it in Texas, during my fourth year of residency. I wrote mostly because I missed home. Missed Hawaii. About four years later, after almost dying, it felt important to continue. I had more to say. But I was too tired. For now, finishing it would remain a little dream.

However, during the month of zoning out in front of the TV, hooked up to a hundred-foot-long plastic tube connected to an oxygen tank, I did think about it.

In places like Kahaluu, we were taught Hawaii things were best. People on the Mainland could not fight. Hawaii had the best beefers. The food? Screw the Mainland. Try eating a roast pork or chop steak plate, and you'll taste what *real* food is like. *We* had the best weather, beaches, music, and people. God's Country. Though I still agree with some of this, I now think about how the smallness of local culture also held me back. Then there is the lack of curiosity (not to mention modesty) in our pride. If Hawaii is the best at everything, why go anywhere else?

It wasn't until I moved to the Mainland that some of these myths were dispelled. When I went to Nebraska for med school and ate Omaha steaks, I realized chop steak tasted like cardboard in comparison. Think people from Hawaii are tough? While working in Texas, I treated pregnant Mexican immigrants who would birth their children, no epidural, just grunting, never screaming or complaining. When I traveled to places like New York, I ate at Italian restaurants that killed that little hole-in-the-wall Italian joint in Kaneohe that my parents still declare is the best Italian food on the globe.

Though there were plenty things about the Mainland I found easy to hate, Hawaii things, it turned out, didn't always come off so well either. In fact, don't be shocked, but we were not always the best.

Anyway, when I started this book years ago, it first took the form of a rant that ridiculed both my Hawaiian and haole culture. Remember, I was crabby. A Hawaiian boy living in the middle-of-nowhere, brown-foam-beach Texas, working over a hundred hours a week inside the claustrophobic world of a hospital. Ranting about Texas and the medical resident experience was therapeutic. I can tell you that Navy Seal training sounded more appealing when compared to working on a gun shot victim after being awake for thirty hours straight. But ragging on Hawaii came surprisingly easy as well. The cost of living. The lousy pay, for everybody, even and especially doctors. The thought of my old friends, most of whom had never lived anywhere else, talking like Hawaii was some kind of highly cultured tropical utopia compared to the rest of the world.

I'm not particularly proud of my thoughts during this period in my life. They're unfair and lacking in compassion; but I can't totally disavow them, either, years later. During my month in recovery hooked up to oxygen in front of the TV, I found myself in the middle of an Anthony Bourdain *No Reservations* marathon. The Hawaii episode was squeezed between one set in Singapore and another in France. Pulling a pig from an imu and chicken long rice looked drab and tasteless in comparison to red chili crab and white plates scribbled with Bordelaise sauces. It reminded me of what I had been writing. Angry rants about Hawaii fueled by sour grapes.

In truth, I'd really missed home, and showed it by attacking the place I loved. That's how it goes sometimes, when you're both missing and disappointed in something, somebody, and especially in yourself. I wanted Hawaii to live up to itself. I wanted to live up to myself as a Hawaiian. And living in Texas I knew how far away I was from that ever happening.

But now, after nearly dying, writing angry, being angry felt like a waste of time. Sure, anger has its uses. After being laughed at when I'd said I think I'm going to be a doctor, anger set me on my path to med school. It fueled me through my undergrad GPA resurrection: reject good enuff, don't be a panty. Anger at being put on the UH med school waiting list made me do the smart thing and take the full-ride scholarship and move the Mainland. Anger, which is normally not considered a positive emotion, can move you forward if you manage it. If you channel anger into something productive, and not, say, walking around grumpy or punching people out, it can be a get-shit-done universal wrench.

However, after dropping forty pounds in the hospital and almost leaving the rest there in the morgue, I wasn't up for anger. And there are so many other, better tools to reach for before anger. I started to think about what I would say if I had a chance to talk to a kid who was growing up the way I had.

I thought of something my friend Chris had said. He'd gone on to write novels, because, he said, there were few books that showed the lives of real Hawaiians, or of the neighborhoods like the one we grew up in, away from tourism and Waikiki and fancy gated Kahala compounds.

I realized I wanted my book to be about what is possible. Not anger. Not "ainokea." That despite what their neighborhoods teach them, Hawaii kids know they have options. I was never a genius. I don't have a photographic memory nor was I born a math, piano, or football virtuoso. In fact, when it came to academics, for years, I was a terrible student and barely graduated from high school. When I took Latin in college, Latin, in fact, looked like Latin. Science textbooks might as well have been written in Greek. The only thing I was super good at was what I was doing now. Laying down in front of the TV for hours on end. I never thought of it as a skill, but to this day, when I do it, Lynn looks on in amazement. She even asked once, "How do you do that?"

So okay, as a kid I was a couch potato virtuoso. That's a start.

After my illness, I slowly began to regain strength and made it to my son's preschool graduation, my first public appearance. Still toting cane and portable oxygen tank, I walked from the parking lot to the auditorium. I noticed how people gave me a wide birth as if near-death was contagious. But I *had* to be there. Me overcompensating once again, making sure I made my kids' functions when I could. Preschool graduations, football games, student-teacher conferences—my Dad had missed all of mine. He'd always been working or resting after work, and at times, I resented him for it—until, during the first few years of parenthood. I realized I was just like my Dad, practically living at work, hardly seeing my kids. Who kept working when his wife hemorrhaged after childbirth and barely survived? That was me. When our newborn son contracted salmonella and barely survived, where was I? Working. Toughing it out.

As I watched this group of little children tug on their sleeves, struggling to sit still, I wondered how many of them would make it out of Hawaii. I wondered how many of them, for better or worse, would turn out like their parents. I thought about how many of their parents would mistake toughness for the bravery to follow a higher path, choose a more ambitious life.

You see, I think our kind of stoicism and fatalism is both a weakness and our strength. There's a reason I ignored my symptoms, even though I was a doctor. Me refusing to let my wife pick me up when I could barely drive, me arguing against going to the emergency room even though I'd never felt as sick in my life, that's my Dad. He wasn't playing a role. When ninety percent of your people are wiped off the face of the earth in a little over a hundred years, you have to have been been tough to survive. And really, really lucky.

Thankfully, Puana luck struck once again and illness didn't end me. As my son's name was called and he received his colorful preschool diploma, he was beaming. Unlike his grandfather and great-grandfather, always smiling, this kid. He wasn't as tough and, thankfully, he didn't need to be. But hopefully, he'd be as lucky.

One word kept popping up in my head while I watched my son's ceremony, then thought about the book stored in the computer upstairs:

Kuleana.

"Kuleana" is a Hawaiian word that, like many other Hawaiian words, does not translate well in English. Literally, it means "responsibility," but there's a spiritual vibe to the word that suggests an invisible bond between living things, and a person's responsibility to care for what he's connected to. I'm not especially spiritual or culturally sensitive—maybe you've noticed?—but there it was. While I thought about my grandparents, my parents, my sisters, my wife, and my children, there it was. I thought about my past patients, most of them Stage Four cancer victims who clung then slipped from life. I thought about my friends and my time on the Mainland. I thought about Hawaii.

I thought about the fact that I *should* have died.

I thought about how my life has been one long-shot bet after another. To have so much luck, to overcome so much, what did that mean for my kuleana to others? I thought about that.

Age six: diagnosed with a rare form of leukemia. Survived that.

Age seventeen: wanted to be a diesel mechanic. Diesel fuel prices skyrocket, crushing the industry. Went to college instead (thank God).

Age nineteen: attended the University of Hawaii. On academic probation with a 1.8 cumulative GPA.

Age twenty-five: after busting my ass in school, offered a $200,000 scholarship by Creighton Medical School. The only full scholarship the school granted that year.

Age twenty-eight: invested in penny stocks. Made a killing and sold off the stocks to buy my girlfriend an engagement ring. The stocks crashed the next business day.

Age twenty-eight: on a whim, decided to specialize in anesthesiology. Salaries for anesthesiologists skyrocketed soon after. Anesthesiology programs became so competitive a year later that there's no way, if I'd waited, that I would have been able to get in.

Age thirty-three: turned down a huge salary and decided to get certified in critical care. Everyone thought I was crazy. Maybe it was my reaction to my wife's hemorrhage the same year, followed by our boy's illness—making it a first, uncertain attempt to sort out my kuleana. Not to just be the cool and distant anesthesiologist raking in the money, but to make more of a difference in people's lives. At any rate, a year later, MD Anderson wanted a young doctor with both surgical and critical care credentials to run its critical care unit.

MD Anderson, one of the very top cancer centers in the world. Ranked with New York's Sloan-Kettering, with the Mayo Clinic. Some even say it is the best. There I was, the kid from Kahaluu.

And yet, only a few years later, age thirty-seven: after all that good luck, I should have died.

But I got lucky once again. The question I now faced was what was I going to do with it? How could I make sure that I wasn't going to waste all that Puana luck?

As Lynn and I drove home with the new Puana preschool graduate and his younger sister, I thought about all the things I would need to teach them. That, yes, Hawaii is great; however, there's a big world out there worth seeing, worth experiencing. Though they'd never be pulled from school to jack up a house to add a story or dragged every weekend forty miles out into the Pacific Ocean, they needed to learn the value of hard work. They needed to learn how to man up, take charge of themselves, and trust their instincts. They needed to learn that good enuff may actually have been good enuff back in the days when housing was cheap, food could be caught, and unions were strong. But those days were over.

From me, I hoped my children would learn, especially my son, that reading and studying does not make you a panty. Reading and studying in med school was the hardest thing I'd ever done and will ever do. Being able to bench 400, choke someone out, or work construction—learning to do these things is laughably easy in comparison. I learned all three at one time or another over the years. Staying up for over twenty-four hours straight, studying for a test you feel you're doomed to fail, doing this for not just weeks or months, but for years, that takes toughness. Wearing a florescent green long-sleeve to work, saving up for a lift kit, drinking green bottles till the sun comes up—there's nothing wrong with this—but don't sell it as toughness, don't sell it as being a real man. A real man does the hard thing even when he knows he might fail. And he doesn't bitch and moan when he does.

I'm not claiming to be the most manly guy in the world (I still bitch and moan with embarrassing frequency); however, don't tell me that studying my ass off made me less masculine. It's as insulting as telling me that my red hair means I'm not Hawaiian.

Like my father before me, I learned that going through life and simply hunting for first-round knockouts is easy. Participating in twelve-round triple-card fights and getting up every time you've been knocked down, that's hard. My dad, thirty years of crawling out of bed at four a.m. to keep his seven-day work-week streak alive, that's tough. Working the tale end of a thirty-six hour shift, so tired that you want to push the patient off his gurney, lie on it, and take a nap, but you save his life instead. Pretty tough, too.

I will tell my children this. Just like everyone else, they have choice. They will rise only as high as hard work will take them. The difference between success and failure is not based on how well they do on the things they enjoy. It's based on how much effort they put into the things they don't enjoy or downright hate. And the great thing about hard work is, unlike calculus, fastballs, and piano playing, we all start with the same amount of talent in it. Many times during med school, I felt flat-out dumb. But I worked, especially on the stuff that bored me to tears. Add some luck, and success in life is almost as simple as that.

How will I know if I've gotten through to my children? I guess I won't find out until they're teenagers and it's time to venture out. Maybe they'll go deep into the fight, maybe they'll get knocked out in the first round. Either way, home will always be here waiting for them if they decide to return, just like it was for me.

But sooner or later they'll have to pick themselves up and go out there to fight again.

Chapter Five

Hoomaunauna Aina (Wastelands)

During our first year of residency, all the medical students read a book titled *The House of God.* The satirical, semi-autobiographical novel was written over thirty years ago and is about a resident who endures long, sleepless hours; cruel, old sages; has affairs with nurses; and is nearly driven mad by the entire experience. We did not read the book as satire.

In many regards, it felt real. However, as we began our residencies, times were changing, and the book was getting more and more antiquated. For example, nurses didn't want to have sex with doctors anymore, especially first year residents. There were still some cruel sages, but human resources began putting leashes on many of the old timers. Doctors, once gods who could never be questioned, now could not give a patient Tylenol without them Google-searching possible side effects. The overall mood of the hospital was being transformed from a military-like environment with an indisputable chain of command to a giant group hug.

However, the hours were still brutal. Residents were considered slave labor. After I'd finished residency, Congress would pass a law stating that it was not safe for doctors to work more than eighty hours a week. (That's not safe for the patients, as well as the doctors.) During my time, there was no such law, and we worked one-hundred-and-twenty hours a week, individual shifts thirty-six to thirty-nine hours long. Medical schools justified the long hours by saying that this was the only way potential doctors could learn all they needed to in four years. But when good cases came in at three in the morning, on my twenty-third hour of work, it often felt as if I was driving drunk and steering with a scalpel. On one hand, this rigorous training was good—to this day I can work a thirty-six hour shift, sleep for four hours, then do it again. However, also to this day, I'm still trying to catch up on all the sleep I'd lost.

And I have to say it does something to your priorities. A lot of your future life will depend on the reward system that you use to get you through those weeks and months of no-sleep, and you don't even know it. There's a reason why doctors have developed a reputation for arrogance and a fondness for expensive toys like Porsches, ski condominiums and third wives. Most doctors feel they never will catch up on all the life they missed out on.

As young interns, we were probably more dangerous than helpful. The best advice I can give to anyone is never get sick in July. July is when all the noobies come to town anxious to poke patients with big needles. Fortunately for patients, there are nurses. Nurses, especially nurses with over twenty years of experience, are the rabid pit-bull protectors of patients. And during my first month of residency, I quickly learned that pediatric nurses were the ones young doctors feared the most.

The House of God never mentioned pediatric nurses. If I had written the book, pediatric nurses would've had an entire chapter dedicated to them. A storm of maternal instinct, intelligence, experience, and estrogen, these women ran the pediatric intensive care unit (PICU). Before I started my rotation, I'd asked the older doctors about the PICU. Each one told me the exact same thing: "Just don't piss off the nurses."

A little further along in my training, after my short stint at PICU, I also discovered the hospital to be a strange place where healthy people got sick. This sounds stupid because a hospital is supposed to be a place where people go to get better. However, a hospital is essentially a small, confined area packed with the sickest people in a city. All the germs and viruses get together, participate in a super orgy, and create new-and-improved germs that assault immune systems. When I had to tell people that we were discharging them, they would sometimes get upset. I would explain that people who stayed at the hospital for too long eventually got sick. Few believed me, but it's true—and the proof was how often I was sick or recovering.

Being Native Hawaiian, I felt a justifiable paranoia and worried that I was more susceptible than most. A huge portion of the Hawaiian population was snuffed out by simple colds and infections. The only reason I am here is that a handful of those people had enough immunity to barely skate by. So at the hospital, it was as if I was walking around with aloha genes. My body was greeting germs and viruses with hugs and flower leis. I once had to do rounds while carting around an IV pole that dripped fluids into me.

Anyway, despite my genetic vulnerability to illness, being a Hawaiian from Hawaii had one key advantage. I understood more accents than anyone else. I was used to hearing the thick, creole, local accents, slurred Japanese-English, and harsh Korean-pidgin. The hospital was filled with staff from all parts of the world. Even though we were in a small town like Temple, people from India, Japan, Mexico, Thailand, and Russia congregated here to learn medicine. Some people liked me simply because they didn't have to repeat themselves to teach me something.

However, the Texans, and there were many of them as well, didn't understand us unless we talked like Yosemite Sam. And they were proud that they hailed from the state that to me was the closest thing to its own separate country. Often, they snidely referred to a strange type of haole I'd never heard of before. They called them "Northerners." Apparently, I was a Northerner because I'd moved here from Nebraska. I was also told that I had a strange accent, like I was from Africa or something. With the Texans, it was the first time in years that being the red-headed Hawaiian lacked advantage. It wasn't good enough to be able to pass as haole here. To be accepted by these people, I had to be able to pass as a Southerner or a native of the Lone Star State.

Opportunity came early one morning during grand rounds. A grand round was a meeting doctors had once a month to discuss how we residents screwed up yet again. This was a great chance for older doctors to pick on younger doctors. It was here where people earned a name for themselves, usually not a good one. As residents, our goal was to get through all four years without having something named after us:

"Holy crap, you just did the Kraus, you idiot!"

I never met Kraus. He'd been long gone when I got to the hospital, but his legend lived on.

Grand rounds were usually brutal. Things often had gone wrong in the operating room and intensive care unit over the course of the month, and during grand rounds, someone had to be blamed. The notion that every time someone died it was someone's fault was ridiculous, but as residents, we bought into it. We blindly assumed that the older docs knew what they were talking about.

So we let them degrade us even though second- and third-year residents knew more than any other doctor in the hospital.

Why was this? Because by our second and third years, knowledge was medical currency. If staff knew we were smart and always had an answer in a pinch, we could get away with anything. So we gorged ourselves with medical knowledge. Also, if we didn't know the answer to something, we would be publicly ridiculed, or even worse, sent on brown patrol. Brown patrol: search for anyone who needs a rectal exam.

But the main reason why second and third year residents knew more than the old timers was because once the older doctors became board-certified, they didn't have to take any more tests or prove anything to anybody. They hung their diplomas on their walls and simply stopped looking stuff up. And since medicine is a science, our human knowledge of it constantly evolves. The last thing some of these old geezers had learned was leaching.

One of these old timers turned to me as I shuffled into a grand round session. "Doctor Puana," he said, "Why don't you explain to Doctor Perales how he killed this lady."

Great. He was turning it over to me so that he could 1) pit me against another doctor—they enjoyed watching us tear each other apart 2) maybe show the rest of the class how stupid I was if I didn't know the answer 3) avoid fielding a question that he did not have the answer to 4) learn about a modern technique without doing research. I had no doubt that if I didn't have the answer, he'd simply turn to another resident and ask the same thing.

I was grouchy and dead-tired. I'd just helped treat some idiot who put a firecracker in his mouth and lit it, blowing his cheek off his face. I also hadn't seen my wife in a week.

But I answered the question. The old man, notorious for his laziness, turned to the rest of the doctors. "Are we going to trust that answer from a Yankee?" he said.

I was too irritated to eat the Yankee thing for the hundredth time. "I'm from Hawaii," I said. "I grew up a lot more south than you did. Hell, I call some Mexican northerners. Who's the Yankee now, haole?"

Thankfully no one knew what "haole" meant, but it felt good to say. To Texans, the more south you were born, the more true-blooded American you were. So in a way, I was questioning the old doc's patriotism, too. The room was silent. People couldn't believe I'd just back-talked the chief of surgery.

But the old doctor was so taken aback he had no rebuttal.

No one bothered me after that.

Lynn was deep in her own residency, of course, during this time. Imagine two people sleepless to the point of psychosis; now imagine them married to each other. What were we thinking? The answer: we didn't have time to think. That's what spared us.

Our time off rarely overlapped, which was also bad. I was depressed and grumpy and craved the company of someone, anyone who could fill this void. Thankfully, I soon discovered that Brian, my old friend from the University of Hawaii, the one who had taught me how to study during undergrad, lived close by on a military base. We would spend what little free time I had taking my boat out wake-boarding.

My luck improved further when I met Bill, a fellow resident at the hospital.

In Hawaii, the natives I grew up around were often called kanakas. Though kanaka simply means "person" in Hawaiian, it's also a word used to describe country bumpkins who like to drink and get into fights, guys like the young version of my dad, basically. Bill was from Louisiana, and people from that state were the kanakas of the South. Bill was not an ocean lover or diving fanatic, but he had his points, such as growing eating raw foods, roasting pigs, and speaking Creole pidgin. He was raised in a rural, dirt-poor neighborhood surrounded by livestock, guns, and broken-down cars. His people had a love for their land—we're talking about those folks who refused to leave the when Hurricane Katrina hit. Bill the Cajun was the Mainland version of me.

He was a talker, like me. He'd also spent a large part of his life "passing" like me. We both knew when to act haole and when we could let our guards down and be ourselves. We were also older than most residents—our paths to medicine longer and more twisted.

With guys like Bill around me, and Brian nearby, the thought of spending the rest of my life in the Mainland no longer made me physically ill. I could live here, I thought. Lynn and I used the money we made from flipping our house in Nebraska and bought a home in Holly Oaks. The house sat right next to a man-made lake as big as Hawaii. Later, during our second year of residency, Lynn got tired of the house and wanted a property big enough to raise horses. We sold the Holly Oaks house and bought a vacant one-hundred-and-eighty acres in middle-of-nowhere Texas. Lynn wanted a barn, and I wanted a gun range. Lynn also wanted two houses built on the property so her parents could move from Nebraska and live with us.

We were growing roots and making plans. Unlike other medical residents, we were using our occupation to full advantage when it came to applying for bank loans. (Be careful what you're good at.) I had the wife, the house, the career, so now it seemed the only thing left was the kids. Without much thought about where we'd find the time, we decided to start our own family. Lucky so far in everything we'd ventured, we were sure we could juggle anything life threw at us.

3.

I liked kids. In fact, when I said I wanted, like, twenty of them I was only partly joking. A slight exaggeration. Fortunately, Lynn was actually agreeable. Unfortunately, her body wasn't. At first, Lynn wouldn't get pregnant, and I found myself collecting sperm in a cup. Then, when she finally got pregnant, she had a miscarriage. Over the next couple of years, three more miscarriages followed. It turned out that her grandmother and great grandmother had both died birthing children.

The disappointment was very hard, and I was anxious to do my best to be supportive. Hence agreeing to the houseless one-hundred-eighty acres where she could one day raise horses. Hence the three German Shepherds and one fat cat. And the biggest "hence," accepting her solution to our housing problem.

She called to tell me she'd found us temporary living quarters, and wanted me to meet her at the property in an hour.

I arrived and waited. After several minutes, I saw her driving toward me, talking on her cell phone. She was towing a giant, one-hundred-and-eighty-five- square-foot shoebox with wheels. The trailer was off-white with ghastly gold stripes along its sides. I couldn't believe it—we were officially white trash.

Lynn pulled up to me, smiling, excited. She walked me through the entrance, which was as small as a port-a-potty door, and gave me the tour. The trailer consisted of two big windows and cheaply made walls that shook when I closed the door. I felt as if I'd just walked into a coffin. Lynn bounced up and down like a little kid and said, "Watch this. You'll love it."

She pushed a button on the wall above the combo stove-oven-microwave-washing machine. There was a whirring and a shaking. Half of the wall on the other side of the trailer began to extend outward. The operation probably added six more inches of room, total. The extension left a crease on the floorboard that I would constantly trip over for the next six months.

I wanted to find the salesman and kill him.

This thing was cramped in every way. The bathroom was so small, I got bruises and pulled muscles from trying to wipe. To make matters worse, we had no sewer system. There was no gauge or warning light that informed us when the septic tank was approaching full. Instead, the indication of a full tank was quite abrupt. When the tank filled, the trailer's toilet bowl developed something like gastric reflux. If the tank was not taken care of immediately, the trailer would fill with sewage, so we had to immediately stop everything were doing and empty the tank.

Emptying the tank meant attaching a long corrugated tube to the side of the trailer then sticking the other end of the tube in a deep, lined hole powdered with lime. I would have to close all the windows, lock up the dogs, and unleash the fury. It didn't matter what time it was—sometimes it'd be a hundred-and-five degrees outside, and I'd be emptying that septic tank retching in God-awful disgust. On other occasions it'd be in the middle of the night, and I'd be outside sniffing in the most horrific smells I'd ever encountered. It had to be done every few weeks. I might just as well stayed home in Kahaluu and driven a septic tank pump-out truck.

So there we were, three large dogs, one cat (who hated the dogs), and two humans living together in the middle-of-nowhere Texas. As for our belongings, they sat in a Matson shipping container right next to our trailer. Also Lynn's idea.

I put the trailer on blocks and began to build a fence for the dogs. I sure as hell wasn't going to have those pets living in the shoebox with me. An hour later, it started to sprinkle. Then, it began to rain.

It wouldn't stop for four months.

Three months into trailer living, I came home from the hospital, and our half-mile driveway was washed out—again. I was soaked, tired, and hungry. I glanced at the dog enclosure. They weren't there. I was too exhausted to care.

When I entered the trailer, I saw them. All three wet dogs were packed in the trailer with Lynn, who was crying. Sobbing, she explained that Simba, her favorite, had been standing outside on three paws, pathetically trying to keep at least one foot dry. She couldn't stand to leave the dogs out in the pouring rain any longer. A soaked Simba was comfortably sprawled out on a stack of my clothes.

Like my father before me, I was the man of the house. Like my father before me, I instantly caved. I bit my tongue and hugged Lynn as I took a whiff of the trailer interior. It smelled like an old, wet rag.

Even though Lynn's decision-making could be seen as somewhat flaky on the home front, at the hospital, she was a machine. Medical students would stand in line to go on rounds with her. She would never accept anything but perfection. Even though we were in different specialties, I used to call her in the middle of the night and ask her opinion about my patients. It was like having my own personal consult service. People used to think I was so smart, but a lot of time, she deserved the credit for a spot-on evaluation.

She used to tell me that she wanted to kill my sisters. After all, they were the ones who'd coddled me throughout my childhood. She'd say, because of them, it was as if she was expected to do the same, and was now on-call twice as much. I, on the other hand, could not be bothered on my days off. I'd go hide out with Bill or Brian out on the lake, or I'd catch up on sleep.

Lynn was a star among the residents. She was so good, in fact, older doctors were encouraging her to drop internal medicine and switch to cardiology, a much more competitive and coveted specialty. Lynn finally agreed. She would be the second woman accepted into the cardiology program in Texas A&M history.

4.

As my third year of residency was winding down, I was jaded, chronically tired, and felt like I'd seen it all. Light bulbs pulled out of orifices. Bad ass cage fighters going ballistic in the O.R. Fellow doctors shooting up drugs. I'd even performed CPR on a clown.

I was now a senior trainee. Early on I'd made a fundamental discovery about medicine: Nurses are the backbone of any hospital, and those with experience know a ton about medicine. Once I treated nurses with the respect they definitely deserved, they loved me. It helped that I was easy-going; even if I was knee deep in blood and guts, I'd never raise my voice. Sometimes I'd even joke around with them during an emergency. Humor calms the troops. It also hid my inner terror as patients barely hung on to life.

As a senior trainee, I was also now practicing my chosen specialty, anesthesiology, and if you ask any doctor, he or she will confirm that if the anesthesiologist, who sets the tone for surgery, is sweating, everything goes to hell. Fortunately, God blessed me with inactive sweat glands. I was soon the go-to-guy at the hospital when it came to impossible cases, and I enjoyed the action and respect.

However, with the acres and houses under construction to pay for, I needed to make extra cash. This was because Lynn decided to erect an eighteen-thousand square-foot barn/apartment combo that would house her horses, our cars, and her parents. The Barnominium, as we called it, soon became something of a minor legend in Temple. Rumors spread that some eccentric millionaire built it. People were saying that even the floors were made of glass so that the owner could look down at the bottom floor and see his horses any time he wanted to.

The truth was, we were spending like the millionaires that we weren't. We had our excuse—two doctors, working too hard. We had all the unresolved emotions having to do with Lynn's miscarriages. Each one made a stressful situation more intense, and less able to be "talked out." Who had time to talk? The nearest therapy at hand for Lynn was the creation of a huge monument to her dreams. Hence, the Barnominium.

There's a lesson here for all of us, but especially those who, like me and Lynn, have had to work like dogs for too long. When success is within reach it's easy to go wild. It's like a cork being unscrewed from a bottle of champagne that someone has left in the sun and then deliberately shaken up.

My other point is that these weren't ordinary luxuries we were spending on. They were "projects," which meant they would contribute to our future, which basically meant they could not be questioned. (Lynn still doled out my allowance, after all.)

We now owed a lot more money than ever before, so we supplemented our income with moonlighting trips.

The most interesting of these was when we were hired by a law firm that was filing a class action lawsuit against welding rod companies due to their connection with Parkinson's disease. We flew around the country in private jets and performed neurological exams. After about twenty trips, the firm picked us to go do testing in Hawaii. Really, they only wanted Lynn, but there I was again, part of the package deal. It was great. For the first time in my life, I was actually practicing medicine in Hawaii. It wasn't complex medicine—a Parkinson's screening takes about two minutes—but I was glad to be back home treating my people. Maybe too glad.

Once in Hawaii, the other doctors-for-hire got mad at me. Instead of providing quick, revolving door-like treatment, I started up conversations with anyone I could. The woman who ran the clinic, who turned out to be my uncle's friend's neighbor, was in the examination room with me half the time, and we talked about family, diving, and UH football. I talked to the patients as well, and what were supposed to be examinations averaging a couple minutes turned into twenty-five minute gab fests. The other members of the group were not amused, including Lynn. They had to pick up my slack. Dinner was on me.

Yet, something very important came of this trip. For the first time, Lynn got to meet the people of Hawaii outside of my family. Normally, when we examined patients in the Mainland involved with the lawsuit, they'd be pissed when they'd find out they didn't have Parkinson's. "What about the money?!" they or their relatives would ask. Then they'd fake a tremor, borrow a friend's wheelchair, and come back again. We'd just distract them and the tremors would stop, or we'd trick them into catching a dropping pen.

However, in Hawaii, none of the patients tried this. I didn't notice because I only saw about ten people the whole day. But Lynn and the other doctors were floored. When results came in negative, Hawaii people were crying and thanking them for their time. Lynn was shocked. These patients were actually genuinely concerned about their family members, and each patient was courteous. One man was accompanied by twelve relatives when he came in for his two-minute evaluation. Of course, I recognized him, and his two-minute evaluation turned into a thirty-minute talk story session. I didn't even know the family really, just their neighbor.

At dinner that night, all the Mainland doctors sat, perplexed. I told them the obvious: "We're in Hawaii, what did you expect?"

Even though the Aloha Spirit has been co-opted by tourism, it's actually real. The patients we examined that day were perfect examples. As we took off to return to Texas, I missed Hawaii more than I ever had before. But as a doctor who had another year of residency left, I had no choice but to ignore the sick feeling of once again leaving home.

............5.

It was during my third year of residency that Lynn became pregnant for the fifth time. As the first trimester passed, we were cautiously, very cautiously optimistic. After all, she'd gone through four miscarriages, and not all of them occurred in the first trimester. Lynn's parents were moving from Nebraska and were going to live in The Barnominium (free, trusted child care), and we had another house built so that we didn't have to live in that God-forsaken, one-hundred-and-eighty-five square-foot trailer anymore. Don't ask where we thought the money would be coming from. At that point we were riding on a combination of the arrogance of knowing you're good and the blind faith that something will work out.

Because we were expecting a child, Lynn decided to quit the cardiology program. She stayed in internal medicine. Maybe it bothered her that the money would be less when she started a practice because she also began selling make-up, of all things. She worked for a company called Arbonne (yes, the multi-level marketing make-up distributor), not as a medical consultant or anything like that, but as a ground-floor salesperson armed with only a start-up kit.

To say I thought this was a mistake is a considerable understatement, but I just said, "Go for it." That was always the thing with me and Lynn. We were always making unorthodox, seemingly knee-jerk decisions, whether it was selling a lakeside house and buying one-hundred-and-eighty acres in the middle of nowhere or building a Barnominium. But we always supported each other, even if we disagreed.

Lynn being Lynn, she turned it into a successful business. She won a free Mercedes and a trip to Chile. She was always a terrific salesperson, but add the MD credentials, and hocking the stuff was never a problem for her. She was making more money selling make-up than she was as a doctor.

Our son was born in November 2005 during my fourth year of residency. I'm sorry to report, no red hair. But also, no

Rudolph, no Rudy, and no Sue. My son would be a Sam. The pregnancy had been hard on Lynn, and the birthing process was even harder. The joy I felt from becoming a first-time father, that sort of indescribable, opiate-like mixture of pride, satisfaction, fear, and pure love, was short-lived. Eight hours after Sam was born, Lynn, exhausted from childbirth, looked down. "I think I just peed myself," she said.

She was sitting in a pool of her own blood.

"I don't think this is normal," said the intern, who'd supervised the birth.

I was trained for crisis, but not like this. In true Kahaluu fashion, my terror flipped my anger switch. "Get someone who can fucking spell his own name," I said. "Get Jonathan."

Jonathan was a fourth year resident like me. He was a terrific doctor, and I was relieved when he marched into the hospital room. He proceeded to cram his entire hand up my wife, practically to the elbow. Poor Lynn. No anesthesia, nothing. She was being treated like a barnyard animal.

The problem was, like her grandmother and great-grandmother before her, Lynn suffered from a factor five Leiden deficiency. This had probably been why she had a tough time getting pregnant and carrying a fetus to term, and this was why, now, her uterus had hemorrhaged.

I wanted that uterus out. Anything to save my wife. However, Jonathan assured me that he could save the uterus. I bit my tongue and let Jonathan make the call. I knew I was in no position to give an unbiased opinion.

Jonathan saved Lynn and her uterus, for which I am eternally grateful. However, we were not out of the woods. Sixteen weeks into his little life, we discovered that Sam had picked up a salmonella infection. He was so septic, the nurses and doctors could not find his veins. His life was in immediate danger. Again, the Kahaluu came out in me. I was so scared I was furious.

After four people tried to find a vein without success, I was forced to try. I ran down to my operating room and practically brought the whole thing with me. When I returned, Lynn was crying. Sam looked like a floppy pin cushion. I covered his face and tried to go to work like I did a thousand times before.

My hands shook as his labored cries got weaker and weaker. I grabbed the needle and tried to calm down. I actually started to sweat. I was about to pass the needle to someone else when my mind drifted to one of my old trauma surgeon mentors who'd helped train me: Dr. Red Duke.

Dr. Duke was a hell of a surgeon and even once had a mini-series on TV about his adventures in the hospital. He was an old cowboy who didn't take crap from anybody. He liked me because we were both red heads, and, of course, because I was from Hawaii. (All doctors love Hawaii.) We'd talk about hunting and fishing, and less frequently, medicine.

Dr. Red Duke once told me that the most important thing I had to have as a doctor was confidence.

"Rudy," he said, "you want to say to yourself that the worst thing you can do for a patient is have someone else work on them."

I composed myself and stuck Sam's lifeline in a vein with one try.

As Sam recovered, I could not shake the feeling that my son was like me. I'd passed on my weak immunity. Like me, he'd be confined to hospitals for much of his early childhood. Like me, his aloha genes would be constantly assaulted. Fortunately, days, weeks, and months went by, and he was doing fine. There were no signs of leukemia-like blood disorders, no pissing of pure blood.

The respect that I had for my mother during these times skyrocketed. I'd always thought that I got my calm-in-the-middle-of-a-hurricane, never-sweat genes from my father. The man who built boats, hand-fished forty miles off shore, and sank boats with seemingly zero stress. It couldn't have been from my mother, who'd gone into panic mode when she learned about 9-11 and refused to let my father get on a plane for weeks because she said he looked too much like an Arab, and they might not let him fly. The thing was, he was on the Mainland and she was in Hawaii.

But as I was now thinking about it, when the stakes were high, she had a cool hand. "You just drank too much fruit punch," she'd told me when I'd peed pure blood, before rushing me to the emergency room.

I've apologized to my son for my bad genes. I don't think he knows what I'm talking about. But hopefully he inherited some of the magical stuff from my father and mother, too.

6.

My personal life stabilized, and as a fourth-year resident, I owned the joint. All of us fourth-year residents were cocky and at the cusp of making real money. However, I turned down every job offer thrown at me and decided to do a one-year fellowship in critical care. Other doctors thought I was crazy. Almost every intensive care unit in America had once been run by anesthesiologists, but they stopped doing critical care medicine years ago because it didn't pay. The year I started critical care training, there were about three-hundred fellowship spots available nationwide. Only about forty spots filled. Basically, I was turning down a four to six-hundred-thousand-dollar-a-year starting salary for another year of training that would qualify me for a specialty that demanded longer hours and paid way less. To most, it seemed like a complete waste of time.

Why did I do it? Just like my decisions to become a doctor, to choose Creighton over the University of Hawaii, to choose anesthesiology when it wasn't as popular, to propose to Lynn, to buy one-hundred-and-eighty acres in middle-of-nowhere Texas, to try and have children while still in residency—like all of those fork-in-the-road choices, it was a snap decision that just felt right. Maybe it was out of a sense of adventure, me constantly making choices without painful, Hamlet-like rationalization and self-deliberation. Others, however, including Lynn, were looking at me as if I was that slow child who'd spent days playing in a cardboard box by himself.

Soon afterwards, I became a hot commodity overnight. At about the same time that I began my fellowship, surgeons started to tire of internal medicine doctors taking care of their patients. It wasn't that internal medicine doctors weren't great doctors. I was trained by many of them during my fellowship and would have gladly had them take care of me if I was critically ill, but they weren't trained to be in the operating room. Surgeons wanted operating room-trained doctors caring for their intensive care patients. They wanted to work with doctors who spoke their lingo. My training in anesthesiology provided the surgical experience they were looking for. My fellowship in critical care qualified me to run their intensive care units.

Hospitals were now receiving funding from a national organization called Leapfrog if they practiced safer medicine. They started to offer critical care doctors with operating-room experience way more money. Wouldn't you know it? I was one of the only young doctors around who had the credentials to take on this kind of position.

By the time I was half way through the fellowship, I signed a contract to work at MD Anderson, the largest cancer intensive care unit in the world. They offered a package with a sweet vacation and retirement plan, and it all added up to about a half-a-million dollars a year, starting pay. I was about to become the youngest associate medical director in MD Anderson history.

This meant moving closer to Houston. Lynn and I sold the one-hundred-and-eighty acres and The Barnominium, packed up Lynn's parents and Sam, and bought ten acres in Tomball, Texas. Thankfully, the land came with a house this time around.

My last remaining obstacle was the oral board exam. I would have to sit alone in front of a group of experts in my field who would ask me the most preposterous, never-happen-in-a-million years, "what I would do" questions.

This was the last test I ever had to take, and I studied too many years to let anything stop me now. After seven years of undergrad, four years of med school, four years of residency, and one year of fellowship, I was finally a full-fledged doctor. I graduated a twenty-eighth grader.

Chapter Six

La hoeleele (Dark Days)

.... 1.

My unit at MD Anderson was an immense, fifty-three-bed wing filled with some of the sickest people in the world. We treated heart attacks, strokes, and traumas, everything a normal hospital faced, only our patients had cancer to boot. The normal death rate in an American intensive care unit was about nine percent. Our mortality rate was fifty percent. We took patients desperate for one last chance, patients making a last ditch effort for survival.

MD Anderson was a research hospital. It provided me with my own lab and minions of med students and residents. All of a sudden, I went from student to boss. People asked me for advice instead of the other way around. After all that training, the buck now stopped with me.

Nurses refused to call me Rudy. I was now "Dr. Puana" to patients and staff alike. I understood the need to refer to me as "Dr. Puana" in the company of patients—no one wanted Rudy, the Red-headed Hawaiian, flying in on his sleigh to save the day. The title "doctor" was important—I'd seen heart rates and blood pressures stabilize at the mere mention of the word. As a doctor I was in the unique position where it was socially acceptable for me to assault people with sharp objects. No one wanted a "Rudy" stabbing them. They wanted "Dr. Puana" to do it.

But when I told everyone it was okay to call me Rudy when patients weren't around, they refused. When I asked my secretary to call me Rudy, she said, "Dr. Puana, there are rules we have to follow in this department and that's one of them."

Despite the stiffness, formalities, and long hours, I loved my job at first. I quickly made a couple of very good friends. First there was Karen, a small, full-cheeked Chinese woman who looked like the Asian secretary in the office of every middle school in Hawaii. She moved as if she was wading in a pool of cement. When I'd met her, she had a piece of food stuck to her blouse and her hair was a wiry black mess. Her blouse was untucked in the front and partially tucked in the back. She didn't look like she could operate a telephone, much less the Critical Care Unit. Boy, was I wrong. She was nothing short of Einstein on speed. She talked like an auctioneer and knew exactly what was going on with everyone in the unit without even writing anything down. She'd even remember the name of a patients' neighbors' dogs years later.

Then I met Joe, who was a slender Latin-looking guy with glasses. Most of his hair was lost from years of stress. He was born and raised in Columbia, trained in anesthesia in Israel, went to Australia for critical care, and practiced medicine in America. He was more of a mutt than me. His accent was a mix of English, Spanish, Hebrew, and Arabic. His forte was that he could diagnosis ninety-nine percent of his patients from the doorway without laying a hand on them.

One day, during my first month at MD Anderson, a crowd of doctors stood at a patient's bedside desperately trying to figure out why this patient was actively dying. Joe, fresh from yelling at his secretary about something, swung around the corner and glanced at this patient for a split second from the hallway. He looked at me as I too was on my way to help and said, "Hold a second, hold a second, vait heer." He stuck his head in the room and said in his thick Hispanic/Hebrew accent, "Dis men gots a hole in hiz lung. Puts a toob in hiz chest."

He was right, and everybody knew it once they translated what he'd said.

Another huge positive of the new job, besides working with Karen and Joe, was that I didn't have to deal with operating room politics, where two doctors were always working on one patient, and disagreements caused egos to collide. In intensive care, I was on my own—no arguing, no compromises. Other doctors stayed away, because quite honestly, they did not want to take care of these patients. Even doctors don't want to have anything to do with death, and the intensive care unit *was* death.

When I paused to look around me, it sure looked like I'd finally made it. Rudy the Red-Haired Human was now Dr. Puana, genius in charge. Teams of bright, driven people reacted to my slightest criticism or off-the-cuff suggestion. I had the support of the largest cancer research hospital and all those resources were at the service of people who truly, desperately needed my help.

So why did it all go wrong?

Well, first there's death. At my hospital, we dealt with death as an everyday occurrence. Death was our starting point; people came to us because they were dying. Sometimes we succeeded in saving them; much more often, we failed. It wasn't long before I started to feel like a doorman at an exclusive club, the guy who decides who to let past the velvet rope.

Chemotherapy was one of our biggest weapons against death. But it was also, too often, its precursor. Basically, with chemotherapy, we just poison the body and hope the fast-dividing cancer cells die first. That's why we do rounds or cycles of chemotherapy. We try to kill as much cancer as we can until the body can't take it. Then, we let you recover and try to kill you again. All that research and those forty-pound brains hard at work, and the only thing we still have is poison. A hundred years from now, it's entirely possible people will think we were insane for coming up with this treatment. But right now, it's all we have.

At MD Anderson, as at any hospital in the Western world, sometimes we don't know when to stop. At times, the only hope for patients is for us to give them so much chemotherapy that it destroys all their bone marrow. Then we try replacing their marrow with a healthy donor's bone marrow. We'll put patients in complete isolation in a plastic bubble, on every antibiotic we know of, and because they don't have any bone marrow to make cells to kill bacteria, the simplest infections kill them. There is no more helpless feeling as a doctor than to know your patient is dying from the common cold. As a Native Hawaiian, I could not escape the reminder of what happened to my entire people—every single hour of every day.

Then there was my assigned role in the MD Anderson army. It was my job to clean up and triage on the battlefield, and wait and watch until, not if, the most simple germs attacked the usual parts first—the throat, stomach and sinuses. From these launching points, they'd spread and devour everything in their path, like nutrient-rich organs and blood. Eventually, they consumed and liquefied the vital organs of the host. Again, I couldn't help but think about how most ancient Hawaiians had died in similar fashion when their immune systems could not fight off foreign germs. Only, back then, the death rate was more like ninety percent.

I often felt completely powerless as people died in front of me. Families lamented over their loved ones; children didn't know why Mom wouldn't wake up. The stench of death was everywhere.

There's a saying: ten years after graduating from medical school, twenty-five percent of what we learned in school is proven wrong. For me, in this intensive care research unit, it was probably more like fifty percent. Most of the time, I had to wing it. There was no high-quality evidence or research studies because most of my patients were on experimental cancer treatments as well as chemo.

When I arrived on the scene, I usually heard something like "Drug 1821-4-25 was given to this patient and now we don't know what is wrong with her."

The patient was usually dying, and we had no side effect profile on these drugs. Despite mulling over details and constantly questioning our decisions, most of the calls my fellow doctors and I made had to be made by gut instinct.

When told they have the big "C," patients typically go through denial, terror, then religious resurrection. Witnessing this cycle did not affect me too badly. But then this case came along, the first case to crush me. His name was Patrick Ink. Patrick was twenty-five-years-old and had a mind full of life and a body riddled with cancer.

Patrick's family was crowded around the bed. He'd battled cancer for years, so his middle-aged parents had been through this song and dance at the hospital before. But they knew that this time it was different. However, unlike most patients in these late stages, Patrick was coherent and oddly content.

In most cases, patients this close to death wrestle with terror. They hang onto every word someone says. They attempt to stretch out every second of existence they have left—which makes perfect sense, since patients seem to know when they're about to die, even before we doctors do.

"Doc, I'm going to die tonight," they'll say.

Then they'll die.

If we were lucky, they weren't conscious when they faced death. Patrick, however, was awake and cogent through the entire ordeal. He looked up at me and asked if I could just make it so that he didn't feel like he was drowning. I told him I'd do what I could.

We talked throughout that last day.

His face will haunt me for the rest of my life.

What always made my job difficult was that I had two jobs. The first was easy and that was saving lives. If patients were going to get better, they were going to get better. I just added ingredients and stirred the pot. The second job was the hard part: letting people die. I would make them as comfortable as possible and let nature take its course. It was unnatural and much more nerve-racking to manage the balancing act of, for instance, taking away the feeling of fluid suffocation without flat-out killing someone. It was like practicing an unspoken black art.

Thankfully, most of the patients were too sick to know what was going on at the end, and their families thanked me for my compassion and my ability to stop the pain. However, Patrick was different; he talked till the end. He was talking about Longhorn football then he suddenly looked at me, like someone tapped him on the shoulder and said, "OK, *pau*, let's go."

He smiled and thanked me like I was a waitress bringing him dinner, and died. He was the first patient to thank me at the end, I mean literally right at the end.

2.

What followed I call the dark days. I started to notice the foulness that contaminated almost everything around me; more and more often; it seemed like all the bad in the world had decided to come out in the open and strut around, and I was the only one able to see it.

A few months after Patrick, a wealthy couple flew in on a private jet. The husband, a man in his seventies, came for treatment. He had surgery, and I was taking care of him postoperatively. He'd probably looked very distinguished at one time, but cancer took care of that. He had a small pot belly and a bag that held his waste coming out of his abdomen.

The wife, his third or fourth, was blonde, blue-eyed, and a six-foot bombshell. She was at least thirty years younger, and she had parts on her that were younger than my kids. She was always perfect. Every morning, she would go to Neiman Marcus to get her makeup, nails, and hair done. She had diamonds the size of walnuts on every finger, and she never wore anything twice, never.

At this point, she was tired and disinterested in her husband's fight with cancer. She was also tired of her early morning fight with Houston traffic to get her nails done. She was disgusted by the whole situation and by him. When the nurse would come in to clean him, she would complain about the smell and say, "He wouldn't want me to see him like that." She'd leave the room. The only other people who visited him were his all-female yacht crew and his brother.

His brother didn't like the trophy wife. As time crept on, the family turmoil slowly escalated as the cancer took over. The patient soon lost his ability to eat and understand simple commands. We started another round of chemotherapy and he developed pneumonia. He was put on a breathing machine with full life support and slowly stabilized. At this point, I was having two separate daily conversations with the family because the brother and the wife could not stand each other. In the morning, I would talk to the brother about options and possible next steps. At night, I would talk to the wife about timelines and when it was going to be over. It was apparent they had different motives.

The wife wanted to end the suffering—hers and his. I could see her side of the argument. This man's quality of life was nil. He was one tenth the man he used to be. At this point, it may have seemed we were just keeping him alive for the hell of it. Sure, she would inherit a massive fortune, but this man also painfully languished near death. As for the brother, he was loving, but also selfish. He wanted the patient to live at any cost, even at the cost of stripping everything human from his sibling. I sensed that there may have been tax or estate advantages to keeping him alive.

End of life treatment is always difficult. In medicine, doctors rarely agree on anything. (The only thing you could get ten doctors to agree on is a tax cut.) On top of that, at MD Anderson there was always the shadow of our *Too Sick to Die* policy.

Too Sick to Die meant that a patient was so sick that we were artificially keeping almost every organ system alive. Heart, lungs, liver, kidneys—they were all being helped out. To *earn* death, the patient would have to show some sign of improvement. Only then would we try to wean him off the support.

At the end, the rich old husband was unrecognizable. He had tubes in every orifice and no signs of life except for very primitive reflexes and a heart beat. Who was right between the wife and brother? Both, neither, I only know that I pronounced him brain dead two months later and pulled the plug.

That's another thing about being a doctor. You hear about all the lives we save. What you almost never hear is how many people we kill. At MD Anderson, survivals were so rare, and the cures we offered were so desperate, that I couldn't help but feel increasingly helpless.

As time went on, I shut down and started to disconnect more and more from the patients and their families. From the outside, things looked great. I was sitting on top of my profession in one of the biggest academic centers in the world. Doctors would come here from every country to see how we operated at such a high level. Movie stars, captains of industry, royalty, prime ministers, sports legends—they were all my patients at one time or another. I had my own laboratory. I uncovered a breakthrough morphine pathway and had the privilege of naming the discovery after my son. I earned a high six-figure salary. Construction had begun on my seven-figure house. I was torn between the Porsche 911 turbo and the Mercedes SL 500; my wife already had her G- 500 Mercedes and said you couldn't beat the ride. But I couldn't make up my mind.

And I wasn't happy.

The thing about success and having it all is, of course, it can turn into as much of a treadmill as trudging to the factory or the docks with your lunch pail in hand. One sign that you're on the treadmill is to think that the solution to everything is more money. I decided to look for a new job and called a good friend of mine I'd met back in residency, Craig Fisher.

Craig was a mover and a shaker. When we were all broke young doctors, he was buying houses and investing in businesses. Rich and single, he used to drive ninety minutes into work because he refused to live in small town Temple while he trained with us. He would globe-trot to places like Brazil and say to administration that he was doing research with some semi-bogus organization. He was also generous with small favors and fixes. If you wanted to get out of something, you asked Craig how to swing it.

So I called him up. He told me about his job, and it sounded great, so he told the powers-that-be to give me a look. If I knew Craig, an endorsement from him was gold. This partnership he was talking about had a line waiting around the block to get in, but I knew all I needed was some face time.

The partnership in Dallas took Craig's word, and with one look at my resume, they offered me an interview. That's when I knew it was money in the bank. So I went to Dallas, and they wined and dined me. I hugged people, kissed babies, and told them that they were the best. I wasn't lying this time, they were. The group was all about money. The leader of the group was two parts businessman and one part doctor, slick and in control. No negotiations needed—I would start at a fifty percent raise from my current salary, and within a year or two, I would be making seven figures a year while working half as much. No brainer. Lynn agreed.

When I went back to work at MD Anderson I told only three people about my deal with the devil: Karen, Joe and Chuck. Chuck was a physician's assistant who knew more about medicine than most doctors, including me. These three were the only ones whom I could trust with such news.

Doctors are especially vindictive if they feel like someone is jumping the queue or showing disrespect. In this case, if the other bosses knew I was leaving after my contract expired, I would be doing twenty-four-hour calls for six months straight. Everyone would be taking vacations until I left.

Karen and Joe were happy for me. Both had switched between private practice and academics before. Chuck approved as well. They were sad to see me go, but they knew this job changed people. They were happy that I thought it was the right move for my family and that I was getting out of the death factory. For them it was different. Karen's whole family was in town, and her husband worked as an anesthesiologist in the same hospital. Joe had five kids and couldn't just pick up and leave like I could. Chuck, hell, he could work anywhere and MD Anderson was as good a place as any for a cruise guy like him.

I'm not sure what I would have done if they hadn't supported me. If they had tried to convince me to stay, I might have. We were doing significant work there amidst all the blood, guts, and tumors. Experimental drugs, experimental procedures, lab work—every death brought us a millimeter closer to treating cancer better. Every life saved felt like a minor miracle, even if that life only flickered for a few weeks or months after treatment.

But I was getting burnt out. I hadn't had one decent month of relaxation and sleep for over thirteen years. The new job in Dallas would make kicking back possible, and it would pay me insanely well while I did it. So with Karen, Joe, and Chuck's approval, I made preparations to bail from the killing fields.

Any lingering doubts were erased when I treated a patient named Simeon.

Chapter Seven

Kimeona (Simeon)

.... 1.

One night, while secretly finishing my tenure at MD Anderson, I was sitting in Pod A, one of six in the intensive care unit. I was called twice overhead: "New admit in bed 10." Then I was paged twice, one thirty seconds after the other. It wasn't an emergency, just the usual bureaucratic mess. The secretary paged everyone, the nurses who received the page paged me again, the secretary from the other unit paged me as well, and they all refused to give up paging privileges because doing so would, in their minds, represent some sort of demotion. Anyway, I stood up and headed for the new patient. I saw a dark-skinned, white haired gentleman with a tracheotomy tube sticking out of his neck. As I got closer, I saw what I needed to see: the *upepe* nose. This guy was Hawaiian.

It's always a powerful moment when two people from Hawaii meet on the Mainland. First of all, you can usually pick a Hawaii person out of a crowd from the way we walk and talk. We also all seem to subconsciously dress local and wear Hawaiian jewelry so we'll be recognizable to each other. Stuck in Texas, I was hyper-vigilant about the signals; I had it down to a science. If the possible local was a woman, I would immediately look for a gold Hawaiian bracelet or pendant. Jade was a big giveaway. If it was a man, I would look for a Honolulu Police Department tee shirt or Scott slippers. Once I would spot someone who looked the part, I would close in. "Where you from?" I'd ask. They would tell me they were from Pearl City or Waimanalo, and I would tell them I was from Kahaluu. Then the pidgin would begin.

The older folks always smiled. They automatically knew I must have taken a beating growing up in Kahaluu looking the way I did, and once they heard my last name, most of them claimed to see the Polynesian facial features. The young ones would hear Puana, tilt their heads, squish their foreheads and say, "Isn't that Hawaiian?" They couldn't see past the red hair. After the small talk, we would then engage in the one thing that I missed most of all: a real retro Hawaiian hand-shake.

Locals had the whole hand-shake thing right. On the Mainland, a hand shake was a test of strength. I thought I was getting mugged during the first hand-shake I got on the Mainland. I guess Mainland people think that a firm hand shake confirms their dominance over the universe or something like that. In Hawaii, it's casual except for the popping sound on contact, if perfectly executed.

Every meeting of a local up here in Texas was always a pleasure, like seeing a friend at the mall back home only times ten because I'd been away so long. I automatically just wanted to offer a helping hand, dinner, directions, or just an ear to listen. I'd know the other person's home town, nationality, and high school alma mater within a minute. Just like back home.

So when Simeon first came in I felt like hugging him. Not only was he from Hawaii, he was Hawaiian. But he was sick. The cancer had dulled his tan and weakened the big, strong hands that had obviously seen their fair share of physical labor. I'd been in the business long enough to know a fight and this was one.

The evidence of Simeon's showdown with his disease made me want to get right down to work. I first made sure the ventilator settings were correct. Then I worked on the drugs. I had my own concoction of feel-good drugs for my patients. The nurse, a veteran who knew my routine, grabbed what I needed without even asking. She gave me a large needle that was definitely going to hurt and started the drugs. I knew he'd already suffered through a lot of pain, so I made sure he wouldn't remember anything about tonight. As I covered his face so that I could insert a large catheter in his neck, I couldn't help but notice a peaceful silence in the room. I only heard the steady bleep of his heart rate monitor confirming that he was getting comfortable. As I plunged the needle into the side of his neck, a dark red gush of blood filled the syringe. I stared at it for a second; it was dark and warm, which reassured me. I hit the correct mark, and I calmly finished the procedure.

I removed the towel from his very Hawaiian-looking face. He reminded me of my grandfather as a younger man. I imagined that he had a big heart and soft side just like Pops, a big old teddy bear.

After I stabilized him, I told the nurse to get his family. Even with the mechanical ventilator, IV drips, chest tubes and monitors, there was usually enough room for the nurse and all the family members in the room. But this was a Hawaiian family. Hawaiians travel like very few people in the world. I knew that there would be a swarm of family and friends that made the trip, so we cleared space. I was not surprised that an hour later the room was filled with mountains of muscle. One son in particular was gigantic. He played football for the Kahuku Red Raiders (he's now in the NFL). It made me glad my high school football team wasn't ever good enough to play Kahuku.

Situated in the midst of all this was a small Caucasian lady. Simeon's wife. She was quiet and gentle but easily controlled this room full of brute strength. Definitely in charge, she conducted herself with poise and was comforting to the family and even to me. It was like talking to my mom. She even told me that she had a red-headed grandson going to school in the Mainland, making them proud.

I assured the family that Simeon would be okay overnight and gave them my cell phone number. For a physician, rule number one is never give your personal number to anyone. You must have a firewall protecting you at all times because when it's a question of health, people will call you any hour of the night. I had a layer of medical students, residents and fellows, followed by a pair of guard dogs, a receptionist and an assistant, to create the firewall that could stop people from getting hold of me.

But with this family, it would have been a sin if I didn't give them my number. Besides, I knew they would only call if they really needed me. That was the Hawaiian way.

Simeon recovered quickly in ICU despite the fact that intensive care units contain the sickest people in any hospital. The ICU is a contagious breeding ground, a place to catch your death. And, ironically, it was the most expensive place to stay, too. I raced to get him out of the intensive care unit and to a regular hospital bed.

Not that a regular hospital bed was the safest place in the world. Though less dangerous germ-wise, it employed less experienced nurses and lacked the around the clock attentiveness that ICU provided. So when it was time for Simeon to leave, I was relieved, but still scared. The wards are a nebulous part of the hospital where too many are left fending for themselves.

To help prevent clots Simeon's bed was an undulating air-driven mattress. The first time I visited, his wife told me that it was not working. I checked it out; they were right. "We asked the nurses to change it before," Simeon's wife said. "But things don't move like they do in your unit, Dr. Puana."

As an ICU doctor, I knew that what looked like a minor malfunction to the family could have killed Simeon. Also, if there was an emergency with him on a broken bed, there was no way I could have gotten to his airway in time.

I said goodbye to the family and headed straight to the chief administrator. I mentioned the two words that made everyone in the world of medicine stand to attention: death and lawsuit. The bed was immediately fixed.

Would I have done this for all my patients? Honestly, I probably would not have visited most of them once they left critical care. I didn't leave the confines of my unit often. The wards, filled with trainees, had a tendency toward laziness and general disorder. They irritated me, and I avoided them. But I never had a connection to a patient on the wards like this one with Simeon. It was as if, from the moment I laid eyes on him, Simeon had become the best friend in Texas I'd ever had.

He represented everything that was missing in my life, of course. Not only did he remind me of my own family, his sudden presence forced me to remember what I had been. A kid who grew up in the ocean, a young med student who once volunteered at a clinic in Waianae—hadn't I promised myself that I would go back and help my people? One day, Simeon gave me one of many thank you cards. On the front of the card, there was a picture of him on a flat-bottom boat in Kaneohe Bay next to Chinaman's Hat. He was giving the camera man a big shaka, but that look on his face was transparent: Please get that camera out of my face so I can concentrate on relaxing.

Part of me wanted Simeon out of this hell hole and back home. On the other hand, I knew that medicine, like a loaded gun, was dangerous in the wrong hands. He decided to stay and finish his treatment. I was hopeful for him, but I also knew the numbers.

I knew what he was fighting, and his chances of surviving this round of chemotherapy were bleak. Sometimes, doctors are just over-paid statisticians. Give us a disease or condition, and we'll tell you what percentage you got to walk, get rid of pain, live, or die. When his wife, standing next to him, told me that he wasn't flying home yet, I said, "Sounds great."

I could tell that Simeon, subdued, and looking straight at the ground, wanted to go home. But with such a big, loving family packed with kids and grandkids, he had a lot to lose. Like anyone else, he was scared to die, but he was more afraid of the pain his death would cause his family. So he decided to get more aggressive treatment at the best place possible. I just wished I'd heard him say it.

After a few speed bumps, and a few pounds, Simeon got out of the hospital and started rehabilitation. Like any tough, hard-working man, he did great. I would occasionally see him walking to outpatient infusion clinics to get more poison. He was always accompanied by family, and each time I saw him, he had a hand shake and hug for me. It was always amazing to me how big his hands were but how soft his grip was. I told him that I would call Oahu to make sure everything was ready for him. He smiled, scribbled a note on his paper tablet, put his *iPod* on, and walked away.

That was the last time I saw him.

When he arrived on Oahu, the cancer caused bleeding in his esophagus, so he was quickly admitted to Queen's Hospital

ICU. Then he had a stroke. Even after all that, he called me a couple of times from the hospital to say aloha. Soon, he was allowed to return home.

I needed a break, so I took off to Vegas a few days after my birthday. I was at the MGM with a friend playing craps when I got the call. Simeon's daughter told me that he'd passed. I remember it was March 23, but I don't remember if I was winning or losing. I went upstairs to my room.

I bawled like a baby.

At some point I caught my breath between sobs and looked around. My suite was huge, tasteful and luxurious at the same time. White leather sofas. A gift fruit basket with a bottle of Moet et Chandon champagne, still under its plastic wrapping. Outside the heavy double-paned glass windows, I had a view to die for: the pyramid of Luxor at Mandalay Bay, the pulse of neon signs, the bright fountains of water that shot up periodically—like right now.

Vegas was like some bizarre pinball machine that Simeon's death had just lit up like a jackpot. And there I was, sitting on the edge of my bed, Mr. Too Stressed At Work, Mr. Very Important Doctor, Mr. Seven Come Eleven, separated by choice from my children and my wife on a holiday morning. In this city devoted to the banishment of manners, morals, ethics and remorse, I was having a huge meltdown.

But who was I really crying for? Simeon? He was at peace, of that I have no doubt. He'd also been surrounded by his family, that huge Hawaiian family. For hours and even days, they'd been at his side. You can bet on it. That's money. And yes, here I was, completely alone and by choice. Isolated, tossing dice and flipping cards on green felt tables while hostesses in bunny suits freshened up my vodka and lime.

That's money, too. Rudy at the tables celebrating his birthday.

How dare I cry for Simeon? I didn't have the right. It was an insult to his struggle and his values, his Hawaiian self that he'd never surrendered, or at least not the way I had mine. Because I had given up the struggle and the values. There was no difference between me and any other red-haired man in this casino—and that's the way I wanted it, apparently.

....

When I finally managed to drag myself home, Lynn took one look at me and decided it was a good time to pack up the kids and visit family in Hawaii for what my wife called a pseudo-vacation. She called it that because we never had time to relax and be alone when I went back home. My mom always made us stay at her house instead of a hotel. We could afford Ko Olina or the Kahala Hilton, which is where Lynn wanted to go, but, as I would tell her, my mom would kill us if she couldn't cook, clean and watch the kids at her house.

Mom made sure that everything was in order when I arrived. She had my ice cream, fruit punch, and squid luau dinner ready. My wife constantly reminded her that she'd spoiled me so much that she ruined me.

A couple of days into my vacation, Simeon's family invited me to visit them in Kahuku. But I didn't want them to go through the hassle. Besides, I imagined myself, Simeon's cancer doctor, turning burgers on their hibachi, and all I could think is that it would bring back bad memories for the family. And for me. I wanted to forget Simeon; I needed recharging for the big move.

Dallas was going to be a new adventure for us, but it was nothing we weren't used to. We'd moved all the time. In the span of seven years, my wife and I had lived in seven houses, not including the condo and the travel trailer.

To me, at the time, people who said money couldn't buy happiness were either poor or lived in Hawaii. On the Mainland, cash bought a lot of happiness. During training, when my wife and I were struggling financially, life sucked. Then, when we were making some money but living in the godforsaken trailer, money allowed us take a vacation or buy a raft that put an extra smile on our faces. I say extra because we were blessed overall, but money had the capacity to make us even happier. Sad, but true.

On the Mainland, nothing good was free. If we wanted to do something with the kids, even going to the pool cost money. My dad had visited us one year and got a flat tire. The gas station charged him fifty cents to fill it. He was shocked and ready to go home. "Everything cost something here," he said. "And it's too damn hot, and everyone thinks I'm Mexican."

True. People would come up to him and start speaking Spanish. But he was right. Everything cost money on the Mainland. Disneyland, skiing, Vegas, and Yellowstone National Park—it was all expensive. Hobbies were pricey as well. Over the years, I had gone through just about every hobby known to man, from archery, to triathlons, to bass fishing. The first time I'd hooked a bass, it felt like I was reeling in a hundred-dollar vine of seaweed that skipped on the surface of the water.

Later that day when I caught bigger ones—and by big, I mean, they were the size of the fish my dad and I used for bait in Hawaii—I took them home, excited to cook them. Then I took my first bite. I never went fresh-water fishing again.

After staying at my parents' house for a week or so, it was time to head back to Texas and fish up the seven figure salary. I regretted not visiting Simeon's family, but I just couldn't bring myself to do it.

Before we returned home to Texas, Lynn wanted to take a quick trip to the Big Island. I'd talked it up to Lynn for years. We decided to leave the kids with Mom and fly over.

2.

The Big Island is by far my favorite island. People were still old time Hawaiian there. Things were slow paced and traffic was minimal. I loved the Big Island ever since I'd landed on it for the first time as a young man. It still wasn't as built up as the other islands, and it felt like I could drive forever along the sea. There were great untouched expanses of land with nothing on them but empty lots of grass or dense, tangled forests. It reminded me of my youth.

As a kid in Kaneohe, I would play in the empty fields of California grass. My friends and I would commando through acres of head-high itchy weeds and hide in a small, long-forgotten cemetery. The cemetery was bulldozed soon after and became Windward Mall. That was part of my childhood—watching Kaneohe become the suburb that it is today.

And even though the Big Island was also going though changes via development, it was still not as nearly as crowded as Oahu. During my first trip to the Big Island as a high schooler, visiting my girlfriend, I went to the most southern tip of the United States, Ka Lae, and jumped off a forty-foot cliff and into the ocean. It was an amusement park ride with free admission. The water was cleaner and purer than I ever saw it. Schools of fish swam by while I headed for the ancient, rusty ladder to climb back up.

Later, as a college student, I'd lived in a tent on top of Mauna Kea for a couple of weeks. I volunteered to catch endangered birds and help build a wildlife observation station for scientific research. I still remember when the sun set during my first day on the mountain. It got dark and cold, like God flipped a light-switch. At first, I didn't notice because we were all getting drunk in a lighted tent while planning the hike for the next day. When the lights went out and the bottles were corked, I made my way to my tent and couldn't believe my eyes. It was the clearest, dark blue sky I'd ever seen. "Wait till the moon sets and the stars are the only things up there," my friend, Matt, said.

I decided to wait for the moon to set before I went to sleep and was glad I did. When the moon went down, the stars just jumped out of the sky, and it seemed like I could almost touch them. They were the brightest, crispest skylights I'd ever seen. A long ribbon of cloud streaked across the sky. I must have stared for hours.

For the next few nights, I did the same thing, watched the sky for hours, and I always noticed the same ribbon-shaped strip of clouds overhead. I figured there was some kind of trade wind effect making the same pattern night after night. I finally asked Matt what he thought of the clouds. He looked at me and laughed. "That's the Milky Way, genius."

The friggin' Milky Way. Wow.

When Lynn and I went to the Big Island, it was important to me that Lynn see these things which were really feelings. I told her about the bird we tried to help save, the palila, an indigenous yellow and gray-feathered finch that was decimated from avian disease spread by mosquitoes, and how we relocated them to Mauna Kea because it was high and cold enough to be mosquito-free. I told her about how we'd come down from the mountain looking like a herd of stink vagrants returning from a mushroom-picking expedition. We would wash in the public showers in Hilo and then go eat a hot meal. Hilo was like Kaneohe had been years ago when I was a little kid. Humid, green, and rainy, low-rise offices and outdoor shops, a small movie theater that played films that had been released months before on the Mainland.

When it came to vacations, Lynn and I were usually in synch about where to stay. But not on this one: She insisted on Kona with the nice hotels and the shopping; I insisted on a tent on the beach. We stayed at the Hilton. Her version of compromise.

As a consequence, I was surprised when Lynn wanted to drive from the Kona Hilton to Hilo and check out the hospital there. We drove past eighty miles of blue coast, waterfalls, and red ohia flowers. I wanted to drive down Waipio and walk on the black sand beach, but our rental car didn't have four-wheel drive. Unlike on Oahu, there are actually reasons to own a monster truck on the Big Island.

When we arrived at Hilo Medical Center, our reaction was unanimous: What a dump. The small, three-story, white-and-peach hospital only had three operating rooms, and only one was in use. Hilo, of course, was still old-school, which meant critical care doctors, not surgeons, still ran the ICU. They made way less than I did in Texas. There seemed to be something wrong with each doctor as well, like they'd ended up here because no one else would take them. One was a hippie-type who would work for three months then out of nowhere split to someplace like Borneo for the next three. Some were hiding out from malpractice suits on the Mainland. Another seemed obsessed with Filipino women.

Lynn surprised me again by asking the administrators if there were any openings. There weren't. It didn't matter. There was no way I was going to take a job that paid me about ten percent of what I was going to make in Dallas. Dallas was going to make me a millionaire. Hilo's salary would put me on equal footing, pay-wise, with school administrators or soon-to-retire hotel managers. I did not kill myself studying and taking on one-hundred-and-twenty hour work weeks to be paid the same as a school principal. Regardless, I thanked them and said that if a position ever opens, please keep me in mind. It seemed like the polite thing to do.

We left Hilo, picked up the kids on Oahu, and flew back to Texas. Before we boarded the plane in Honolulu, I dreaded going back. I wanted to stay several more days. Who am I kidding—I wanted to stay several more decades. Of course, it was only when I was onboard a plane that I decided I wanted to visit Simeon's family. From the safety of thirty-thousand feet, where decisions were more like pipedreams lacking risk, pain, and practicality, I imagined buying a house in the same neighborhood and keeping an eye on his grandchildren for him. Maybe watch them grow alongside my kids, and help reinforce the lessons that their parents taught them and mine taught me. Tell them don't let anyone tell you "no can." I wanted to spend evenings sitting in front of the TV while eating kalua pig, real kalua pig from an imu, every night, and wash each bite down with beer. I wanted to see the Milky Way from atop Mauna Kea and jump off the cliffs of Ka Lae again. But, instead, it was time to go home. It was time to focus. It was time to make money.

On the airplane, Lynn offered me the window seat, but I didn't want it. I asked her to close the plastic shade.

Lynn wanted to say something, but stopped herself. She grabbed a crying Gigi, put her on my lap, and told me that everything was going to be fine.

We would soon be off to Dallas with its Amazon blonds, lit-up skyscrapers, and massive GDP. Lynn would be able to buy her acres, her horses, and the kids would get a big city education. I sat in that plane and clenched my jaw while holding my screaming baby because I was determined to do what would make my wife happy. That was the most important thing to me.

3.

We all have relatives whose lives serve as cautionary tales. Maybe it's the cousin who got knocked up at fifteen. Or it's the other cousin who dropped out of high school. Maybe it's the cousin who decided to smoke ice and deal drugs on the side, and ended up getting pulled over with an AK-47 in his trunk. Sentence: seven to ten years.

To me, these stories weren't very useful growing up. It all seemed pretty obvious. Having a kid at fifteen is a dumb idea.

Dropping out of high school: dumb. Smoking ice: dumb. Storing an illegal AK-47 in your trunk? Dumb. Life is short, some kids say, to justify risky, crazy behavior. I think I knew from early on that life is not short. It's long. And people can pay for one screw-up for the rest of their long, long lives.

However, even though I was aware of this, I screwed up as well. Messing up during my first couple of years of college forced me to tack on three more years of grueling academic work. Messing up in high school—I wonder how much easier college and med school would have been if I'd actually learned how to study when I was supposed to.

Anyway, the kind of cautionary tale that resonated for me was like what happened to my brother-in-law Doug. Now, Doug is not in jail, he's not an addict; he is, in fact, a responsible husband with two great kids. But boy, was life sometimes hard for him, maybe far harder than it should have been.

Rualani's husband, Doug was originally from California. He'd moved to Hawaii as a teen and, like me, barely graduated from high school. He hooked up with my sister and instantly became the older brother I never had. We'd hang out all the time, and he taught me how to drive stick in my dad's old beat-up fish truck.

When I was a teen, Doug developed a fascination with photography. No training, no money for classes, the guy would sit there and photograph flowers for hours. When he didn't get the shot that he wanted, he'd take notes and figure out what went wrong. He'd pour over those notes for hours then re-shoot again and again until he got the picture he wanted. He even taught himself how to develop his own film to save money.

Rualani decided to put his hobby to work. They scrimped and saved and opened a studio in Kailua. And with Rualani as the face of the business and Doug as the talent, the business did pretty well. However, no matter how much their business grew, so did the cost of living. Housing and business rental prices soared. Eventually, like many other locals, they saw only one option: pack up and move to the Mainland. They moved to Illinois, where my grandmother, my mom's mother, was living at the time.

Before arriving in Illinois, Doug had secured a Mainland job as a photography shop manager. He and my sister had also bought a house. When Doug, my sister, and the kids got to Illinois, and Doug showed up for work, he discovered that the shop was going out of business.

Scrambling to find a job, any job, armed with only his high school diploma and love of photography, proved challenging. He finally landed employment selling vacuums. Flat broke, he spent that Illinois winter going door-to-door wearing a couple layers of tank tops covered with a Members Only jacket.

After a few months of that, spring hit, and he got a job giving people estimates on sprinkler systems. He then found a side job lifting boxes. None of the jobs provided insurance, and one day, while lifting boxes, he got a hernia. He and my sister had to scrimp and save, empty the loose change jar and their kids' meager college savings, to take care of it.

The day after his hernia was surgically repaired, the local Mitsubishi plant called. Doug had been coveting that job ever since they'd arrived in Illinois and found out the photo shop closed. The union job meant benefits and stability. However, the Mitsubishi guy said that if Doug wanted to work, he would have to come in the next day. Doug had no choice. He jumped in his Yugo (yup, they really owned a Yugo), and showed up. He was greeted by a bumbling man who quickly showed Doug his work area. It was filled with a mountain of boxes stuffed with steel car parts. Doug's job was to move these boxes from point A to point B. Hernia incision aching and pulsing, Doug kept carried boxes while watching assembly line workers push around wing nuts with pencils. The pain began to creep through his inner thighs as he approached a box marked *heavy*. Doug lifted the box. The surgical staples pulled and his hernia popped. The pain melted away, and he continued to work. Mitsubishi kept him onboard.

At this point, Doug's job was good because of the benefits, but it wasn't cutting the mustard money-wise. They had a mortgage and two kids. So against Doug's wishes, Rualani started a daycare. Doug was very reluctant because he knew two things about my sister. One, she loved kids, and two, she couldn't say no. Within a few weeks, Rualani had a couple dozen kids running around her house destroying the joint. She was in hog heaven. If it were up to her, she and Doug would have had twelve kids of their own.

It took a few years to get rid of the house-destroying kids and most of Doug's side jobs. He finally quit the Mitsubishi plant and took another steady job at the airport, and they continued to save. After years of saving and accumulating thousands of miles on that Yugo, Doug and Rualani finally opened a photography studio right next to the local butcher shop. Doug wasn't allowed to quit the airport job because of the money, benefits, and the free flights to Hawaii. But he and Rualani have been in business ever since.

Doug is a hero of mine, so it is weird to say that he's also my cautionary tale. But he is. In fact, my father, who worked hard with his hands all his life, is another hero/cautionary tale. I *didn't* want to struggle like they did. And what the job in Dallas meant, the seven-figure salary, a salary that would also grow and grow, was that I, nor my wife, nor my kids, would have to struggle for the rest of our lives. And as I was sitting in traffic back in Texas, I was resigned to taking the job. What kind of idiot bitches and moans because he's about to make millions of dollars?

As I was driving home from what would be one of my final days at MD Anderson, cars crawled in opposite directions on thirteen lanes. The skyline was its usual smog gray, the overpasses were strewn overhead like concrete spider webs. Bored as usual, I was probably flipping through Houston's seventy-plus radio stations. My phone rang, and I was relieved. Talking to someone, anyone, would make the time move faster. When I looked down at my phone, I was surprised that it was an unknown number with an 808 prefix.

I answered. It was Hilo Hospital calling. They said that they wanted me. They told me other doctors were willing to cut some hours so that I could start full time. I thanked them and said I'd talk to my wife and get back to them as soon as possible. Sure I would: they were offering peanuts compared to Dallas.

They were offering Grape-Nuts compared to Dallas.

When I finally got home, Gigi was crying as usual and Sam was in his high chair. I don't remember what was for dinner, but I remember not liking it because it wasn't Calrose medium-grained rice. White rice was nearly impossible to find in our neighborhood. As I sat there eating, dreaming of rice, Lynn said something out-of-the-blue that I'll never forget.

"If Hilo ever calls," she said. "We'll go to Hilo."

My heart jumped. Before I even knew what was coming out of my mouth, "They called today," I said.

We looked at each other and communicated what I can only describe as a joint, silent sigh. It would be another one of our snap decisions. Just like the trailer, just like the Barnomini-um, just like deciding to buy acres in middle-of-nowhere Texas, we were unified in crazy. Only this time, instead of shifting up and saddling ourselves with more debt, we were shifting down.

We were going to Hilo.

We were giving up millions. We were heading into Doug Country, a place filled with risk, possible struggle, and uncertainty. After dinner, I just had to make sure that we were doing the right thing, so I called Doug. I explained the situation to him and he immediately said, "Take the money in Dallas."

That's how I knew it was time to live in Hilo.

....

My dad is visiting, and yesterday, I decided to take him fishing. It was time for a bit of payback for all those vomit-inducing voyages he dragged me to.

The first step of payback was to not wake up until the sun came up. When we used to go fishing on Oahu, a four a.m. wake up call was mandatory. By the time I got out of bed, Dad was pacing in the living room, already pissed. "How we going catch fish this late?"

"No worry, Dad."

We didn't leave the house until nine a.m.

When I reversed the trailer into the water, it was about ten. Back in the old days, at ten a.m., we'd be forty miles off the coast, and I'd be reeling in slack while puking on the reel. Dad would be hand-lining an ahi or marlin, stepping back and forth, dancing his waltz with his invisible partner. Fifteen-foot swells would be hoisting the boat up then dropping it, and on really bad days, I'd fantasize about the ocean finally sinking us, ending my misery.

My Dad kept looking at his watch. "Frickin' waste time already," he said.

I just smiled and shook my head. He looked out to the ocean. No other boats were out.

"See? Everyone way out there catching fish already."

"No one is out there," I said. "We're early."

Dad thought I was joking.

After we launched the boat and parked the truck, Dad, now running on one kidney, couldn't sit still. I thought about the years of abuse he put his body through. The fights. The bends. The drinking and smoking. The gallons of magic orange degreasing paste he rubbed all over himself, a paste that is now suspiciously off the market. Seventy-three stitches after getting bit up by an ono. The compass fluid he and his buddies drank out at sea. God, this guy was tough. All that, and he'd already almost outlived me.

"How far out we going?" he asked.

I pointed to the nearest buoy.

"Start letting out line," I said.

He looked at me like I was nuts. We weren't even a hundred feet from the harbor yet. But he let out the line.

We got our first strike before we even hit the buoy. Dad was shocked. After we passed it, Hilo still very visible on our right, we caught another one. In fact, for the whopping two hours we were out there, we never even ventured a mile from the coast. We headed back in because we'd already caught enough fish.

As we approached the harbor, I pointed. Other boats were just now being dropped in the water. It was about noon.

"See, I told you," I said. "We were early."

Dad just shook his head. All those years in Oahu having to take the boat beyond marathon distance, hunting for the roughest spots because that was where the fish could be most easily tricked, pushing it to the point where he actually sank a boat named Kathy, the look on his face said it all. He'd been living on the wrong island all these years. It's like I'd told him back in the day when I attempted to build the flashlight holder. Work smarter, not harder. Sometimes that means moving to where the fish are. I'd done it. That was what the Mainland was all about.

"Dad," I said. "You and mom should move here."

He nodded. He was the one who'd convinced Lynn and I to buy eleven acres on the coast, north of Hilo. Yet another house-less lot of land purchased with loan money, but this one smaller and more far more beautiful than the Texas lot, the site of The Barnominium. In fact, Lynn and I hadn't even seen it when we agreed to buy it. It was my dad, on the phone with us, standing on dirt and California grass, telling us we'd be crazy not to purchase. Haunted by the memories of the trailer—the septic tank, the dog hair in my food, and the four months of rain—I wasn't so sure.

But Lynn knew. She knew what would make me happy. This girl, I'm telling you, is one hell of a wife.

So we'd bought it and this time, instead of living in a trailer, we rented a house in Hilo.

When we got home with our ahi, Lynn and my mom were helping Sam and Gigi with their homework. Poor woman. I got to do the fun stuff with the kids. Swimming and diving. Lynn got stuck with waking up early to make breakfast and doing homework.

It was weird, sitting there with my wife, kids, and parents, watching Lynn read to Gigi. My dad had never read to me. We never even talked about a book, not even *Cat in the Hat*.

As if reading my mind, Dad turned to me and said, "Eh, I taught you other stuff."

And he did. Stuff just as valuable as reading. He taught me how to work hard. He taught me never to say *no can*. He taught me that responsibility is doing things you hate doing even when the thought of doing them makes you want to throw up. And sometimes when you do them, they actually do make you throw up, but you do them anyway.

Chapter Eight
Nui Mokuaina (Big Island)

Since I had to finish up my contract with MD Anderson, Lynn took the kids and headed to Hilo a month before me. Fortunately, her parents made the move with her, otherwise she would have been stuck there with only two little kids and the constant night-time croaking of frogs to keep her company.

Although she'd been to Hilo before, she quickly discovered the differences between visiting and living in a place. First off, it was the first time she'd lived where, as a white person, she was the minority. It seemed to her that just about everyone else in this town was Asian or Hawaiian. And the other thing she began to notice was that people seemed to talk and move more slowly than on the Mainland. And they repeated themselves a lot. As a quick-thinking, quick-talking ball of haole energy, just ordering food, for example, drove her crazy. With every trip she took from point A to point B, as she passed each sidewalk-less, rain-soaked yard, she could smell the crack and teenage pregnancy in the air.

The other thing that she began to notice was that if Hawaii is all about "who you know," Hilo was like that, squared. When she first tried to enroll Sam in St. Joseph preschool, he was denied. Lynn had to call my mom, who called the bishop and straightened everything out. Once, after she bought fundraiser laulau tickets from an elementary school, she lost them a few days later. But she figured that since the school had taken down her name when she purchased the tickets, she could just pick them up. Wrong. She approached a large Portuguese woman who was manning the laulau booth. Lynn explained that she'd lost her tickets, but that the school had her name and purchase order on record.

The woman wouldn't give Lynn the laulau. Furious, Lynn walked away. As she did, she overheard a local man telling the Portuguese woman that he'd lost his tickets, too. The two knew each other, and the man received his laulau along with a big hug.

When I arrived in Hilo, I practically kissed the ground for the same reasons Lynn found so annoying—because I was so glad to be home again. To me, Hilo represented what Kahaluu and Kaneohe was when I was a little kid, pre hyper-development. Both places were green and rained a lot. Veined with narrow two-lane roads, both were packed with fruit trees and chicken coops. I was back in The Land of the Lifted Truck.

I was the red-headed Hawaiian again. I stuck out, again. And that was where I belonged.

Unfortunately, I was also significantly poorer.

Dallas had offered me a position that paid $60 a unit. For example, a colonoscopy is worth five units, so that's a $300 job. Open heart surgery is worth twenty-four units, so that's a $1,440 job. Because Dallas is also a big city with well over a million people, there was a guaranteed endless supply of patients.

In Hilo, with its whopping population of 40,000, a stream of open heart surgeries wasn't going to happen. Also, most patients were on state or federally funded insurance, which paid $16 a unit. So I took a seventy percent-plus pay cut. Add to that high state taxes, and I felt like I was in residency again. (This, by the way is why there's a constant doctor shortage in Hawaii.)

So when I got to Hilo, I'd take any case I could find. Lynn and I had major bills. Two mortgages (the empty eleven acres north of Hilo and the house in Texas), rent in Hilo, private pre-school for Sam, and we had just blown a ton of cash on the move. No more gaggle of residents following me, no more personal secretary, no more research, no more private lab—but I was back in Hawaii helping my people, people like the Simeons of the world, and Hilo had some of the sickest people I'd ever seen.

One of the funny things about Hilo is that it's one of the last enclaves of old Japanese men with samurai mentality. They simply refused to go see a doctor. I know, I know, stubborn old men right, what's new? But let me show you what I'm talking about here. Soon after arriving in Hilo, I had one gentleman begrudgingly enter the hospital because his wife would not stop hounding him. I asked him what was wrong.

"Nothing."

After running some tests, we found out he'd had a heart attack five days before. He was only now seeing a doctor.

Another patient, came in, same deal. Wife practically begging him to see a doctor.

"What's wrong?"

"Nothing."

I found an eight-foot long tapeworm inside of him that was probably older than me.

A tapeworm.

Tapeworms are uncommon outside of third world countries. In fact, even when I practiced medicine close to the Mexican border, I didn't see them in patients. But here in Hilo? Tapeworm fest. After a month of practicing on the Big Island, I was half expecting someone to come walking in infected with the bubonic plague.

But that was what it was like. People in Hilo wouldn't come to the hospital unless they were badgered into it. I had patients who were walking in days after they'd had strokes. People coming in with cancers the size of melons.

"What's wrong?"

"Nothing."

Like I said, samurais.

As for the home front, Lynn and I were stressing over money, but Lynn was also still undergoing adjustment pains. Time in Hilo functioned differently than it did on the Mainland. A twenty-year-old story was still fresh.

Once Lynn asked me why people in Hawaii love reggae so much. I told her to listen to the repetitive, slow, casual beat.

That, I said, is the tempo of our lives.

2.

Lynn didn't care for that answer. First off, the tempo of her life was completely different. She lived by beat of some jazz craziness. Also, I'd said "our." A part of her may have been scared that I'd lapse into Hilo-style living, which to her meant, just barely skating by, which financially at least, we were pretty much doing.

So after just six months in Hilo, I begrudgingly took a higher-paying job in Waimea. I'd really liked practicing medicine in Hilo, tapeworms and all, but when the one you love most has the look of financial stress written all over her face, after she'd moved from her sprawling Mainland home to an island in the middle of the Pacific just to make you happy, you take the money. So we packed up yet again and moved forty miles north to a place that in some ways reminded me of Texas. Cowboys, white people, and a segregated population.

On one side, there were poor Hawaiians and locals who had lived here for generations. On the other, there were the rich Mainlanders who reminded me of Steve, my old pony-tailed Resident Advisor from UH. And each side complained about the other behind its back.

"Locals are so ignorant."

"Haoles ruining this place."

"If you're not going to work hard, don't complain about what you don't have."

"I used to have everything I needed. Now everything so expensive, I cannot afford anything."

Of course, when these two types of people bumped into each other on the street, they were all smiles. But when they'd get me alone, as a white-skinned, red-headed Hawaiian, they all felt they could confide in me. It didn't take long for me to start hating Waimea. But it wasn't just the two factions sniping behind each other's back that drove me crazy. I was already missing the rainy green of Hilo. Like all the places rich haoles seem to covet most in Hawaii—Kahala, Kona, and half of Maui—Waimea was dry as a desert. Lynn and I had moved into a cookie-cutter subdivision planted smack in the middle of a flat, grassy field, the kind that can easily be found in Nebraska, Texas, and Anywhere USA.

The worst part was that I was an on-call anesthesiologist at North Hawaii Hospital.

Being a call doc means *knowing* that work can call you at any time, day or night, and no matter what you're doing, you need to be there in fifteen minutes. This means no going out or traveling outside a twenty-five mile radius. It means no pau hana beers. And worse, it means no sleep. Even on nights I didn't get called, I had a hard time sleeping because I expected the phone to ring.

Frank, who was also a call doc at the time, was my bitch-and-moan partner. We decided that we needed an exit strategy. That's when the idea for a pain clinic surfaced. I took my idea to the boss (Lynn). She agreed. Partnering with Frank and his wife, we opened our first clinic in Waikaloa in September 2009. Lynn ran the place with zero employees. When patients did come, her mom manned the front desk.

The clinic was a way to bring medical treatment to the rural, underserved and impoverished populations, which included a lot of Native Hawaiians. Now sick people didn't have to drive three hours to Hilo. But it was also good business, thanks to Lynn.

We started with maybe fifteen or so patients that first month. My paycheck at North Hawaii and what Lynn was making from Arbonne (yes, she was still selling cosmetics, and with all her old panache and success) paid the rent and other expenses. In essence, I was working two jobs now. Just like back in Texas, I hardly saw my kids.

But if I thought I'd seen Lynn function at the highest gear possible, now she somehow shifted into one even higher. If I was working two jobs, she was working four. She executed a full-throttle marketing assault on primary doctors all over the island. We'd take them out to dinner. Then I'd perform lectures on migraines and neck and back pain treatment after failed surgery, stuff I'd learned back when I did my anesthesiology residency. Each month after September, we picked up another twenty or so patients. Many of them, when they saw my last name, were instantly sold.

Over the next six or so months, we moved the clinic two more times. We needed more and more space. When Lynn ran out of primary care docs to pitch on the Big Island, she attacked Maui. By spring, we opened another clinic there. In less than one year, we were operating two pain clinics and were even considering opening a third on Oahu. Without Lynn, I'd still be stuck on-call at North Hawaii Hospital while treating a handful of patients in our first, tiny office space. While I know I've worked hard, in fact, worked my ass off through med school, residency, Texas, Hilo, and Waimea, my work ethic is nothing compared to Lynn's. Work is like breathing to her—if she doesn't do it, she'll die.

But, of course, I was the one who almost stopped breathing. Just when everything was falling into place—the pain clinics were taking off, we began construction on our new house, and it was financially viable for me to quit the on-call position at North Hawaii—I got that 104-degree fever. May, 2010.

....

As I got better, life started happening again. Work, appointments, errands. The slightly tedious repetition that makes life move fast, too fast sometimes. When I had free time, I fished, pounded weights, and flew to Vegas. I forgot about the book, about my sense of kuleana. I really seemed bent on turning into my old man.

I resumed my duties at North Hawaii Community Hospital and worked at the two start-up pain clinics Lynn and I had opened—the one in Waikaloa and one in Maui.

As I worked, getting back into the old rhythm, I felt the effects of my illness. Something had to give, I realized, or I would give out again.

There seemed to be no rational way to quit North Hawaii Community Hospital. Built in 1996, it is essentially a twenty-five million dollar facility kept in the black by millionaires and billionaires who have vacation homes on the Kona Coast. Past donors of the feng shui-inspired forty-bed hospital include Charles Schwab, Michael Dell, and probably the richest of them all, Earl Bakken, the inventor of the pacemaker and co-founder of Medtronic. Basically, any piece of medical equipment that has a battery in it was probably made by this company.

My job at North Hawaii? To anesthetize a bunch of Thurston Howells who needed to be treated for mild old-man infirmities. Gall bladders, appendixes, knees. In most hospitals, nurse anesthetists take care of these minor procedures, but the Big Island captains of industry would accept nothing but a certified doctor to dull their pain. If they suffered sudden, serious ailments, they were flown to Queens Hospital on Oahu by their private jets. So except for the occasional motorcycle accident victim, I dealt with the removal of hairy moles and colonoscopies.

The money was good for such entry-level doctoring, and that had once seemed important. But I'd almost died. Life was too short.

The pain clinics, though also a far cry from the work I'd done at MD Anderson, were satisfying. Essentially, people in pain entered then walked out super happy that they were no longer in pain. And so many of them were local and Hawaiian.

In the end, no contest.

Once I quit North Hawaii, my work day was cut from six days a week to two. For the first time in their lives, I spent time with my kids. We'd go to the beach. I began teaching them how to dive. Gigi, named after my grandmother Genevieve, picked up diving quickly. She'll probably end up being better at it than Sam. Gigi, always with that half-smile, half-smirk that seems to suggest she knows something you don't.

Besides spending time with my kids, I began to golf while the kids were at school, took guitar lessons and then switched to piano. I basically began doing all the things I'd wished I had the time to do as a teenager.

I'll be honest. A part of me does still miss the action at MD Anderson, researching and practicing desperate medicine. During my time in Texas, I'd published articles on thoracic motor paralysis, percutaneous dilatational tracheostomies, and retropharyngeal hematoma formations following blunt cervical traumas (sounds fascinating, I know). It was in my lab at MD Anderson that I gained a bit of notoriety when I discovered that morphine at smaller doses caused less extra-vascular fluid leak; this meant morphine at these doses could be used to physiologically correct the effects of trauma—in effect, using a sedative to do medicine.

Most of all, at MD Anderson, I treated patients who were on the brink of death. It was challenging, heart-breaking work—and a burden and a responsibility. I still feel haunted by, and occasionally guilty over having given it up.

But I knew that being back in Hawaii and having time to spend with my kids was the best thing for me. Finally.

2.

Lynn smiles a lot these days. She's happy, that's the main thing. Her with her three different checkbooks—one for the make-up business, one for the pain clinics, and one personal—she's thriving on the Big Island. And she's made a difference for a lot of local people. If it wasn't for her drive and ambition, there'd be no pain clinics.

And, anyway, what did we give up? A guaranteed sizable income in a land locked city that boasts seven interstate highways and a pro football team. Nothing so great, really. A hustle and bustle lifestyle that would've has us living like, for better or worse, reality TV stars. Who'd want to gawk at some red-headed Hawaiian from Kahaluu, stuck in Dallas with all the cosmetic surgery freaks?

And the funny thing is we ended up doing just fine. The money part is all good. We've got enough, and more. Enough to erect two houses on our eleven acres, one for Lynn's parents, the other with a home movie theater and an underground wine cellar. (I know, doctors and high-technology gizmos, doctors and fine wine.) Enough to have bought another house in Waimea, where my parents will soon live. Enough for Lynn's horses. Enough to send our kids to private school in the state. When we feel like we need a break, we hop on a plane and fly to wherever we want.

All because a big Hawaiian man named Simeon rolled into my ward, saved me from becoming full-blown haole, and reminded me of home.

Sometimes, when I'm strolling on my property, looking out at the ocean, trees, or the pile of gravel that will soon be the foundation of my house, random names pop in my head. Brett (Breath). Marc. Joe. Karen. And of course, Simeon. Oddly, these names are almost never accompanied by images, or even thoughts, just names that float into my head then exit quickly.

Like most people, I do occasionally wonder what my life would have been like if certain events did not occur. What if my dad didn't drag me fishing forty miles out every weekend? What if diesel prices didn't skyrocket in the early nineties? What if Chris didn't laugh at me when I said I wanted to be a doctor? What if Brian didn't teach me how to study?

What if I didn't meet Lynn?

What if Simeon didn't enter my life when he did?

What if I didn't have red hair?

I suppose a number of different things could have occurred. I could have become a trash man like I'd told my mom I wanted to be years ago. Like my old friend Todd or my brother-in-law Doug, I could have entered the workforce right after high school or gotten kicked out of college. Without Simeon, maybe I'd still be in Texas, waiting on a future that included both ex- and trophy wives, getting old and sick, and maybe having a fourth spouse trying to convince a doctor to finally pull my plug.

Instead, here I am, maybe one of the strangest Kahaluu success stories, one that the old neighborhood gossips about.

They do, you know. My parents and friends tell me the old neighborhood sometimes speculates on what made this minor miracle possible. As a Hawaiian raised in an impoverished, rural community, as a red-headed clown who was always more concerned with making people laugh than cracking open books, there's no way I could have endured the ten-plus years of hell it took me to get through college and medical school.

No one ever wants to give me credit, I hear. It must be my parents, they say.

And you know what? They're right. It was my parents. It was my parents, my sisters, the ocean, a boat named Kathy, my friends, my wife, and the community that couldn't make sense of me. It was being exposed to both The Haole Way and The Hawaiian Way at such an early age. The Haole Way taught me to use words to get what I want. To not be too proud to ask for help if I needed it. The Hawaiian Way taught me the value of hard work.

I know that The Hawaiian Way may sometimes means anger and toughness in today's world, but it is still rooted in the tradition of aloha and generosity. Like all poor Hawaiian towns, Kahaluu may have its share of abusers and petty criminals crushed by a sense of futility, but it is also populated by some of the most generous people I've ever come across.

However, there's another factor that must be thanked, and I'd be most remiss not to give credit where credit is due.

The red hair.

It's odd to think that something as mundane as hair color, a source of torment and struggle as a child, helped me achieve my goals, but being the red-headed Hawaiian, torturous at times, the cause of much unfair teasing and bullying, undoubtedly shaped me as well. Without the red hair, I would not have learned to talk quick and sharp as a straight-razor. If I'd had dark skin and hair like my father, maybe the Mainland would have been more difficult to endure, especially Texas, and I'd have cracked.

Either way, I'm glad I got this orange stuff sprouting from my head.

Sometimes it's good to be different.

Glossary

ainokea: a local term meaning "I don't care"

Eddie Aikau: legendary Hawaiian lifeguard and surfer

Gabby Pahinui: legendary Hawaiian slack-key guitarist

hanapaa: Hawaiian slang for "hook up" or "fish on"

imu: Hawaiian underground oven

imua: Hawaiian word for "go forward with spirit"

kahuna: a Hawaiian priest or shaman

kalua: a traditional Hawaiian cooking method that utilizes an underground oven

kanak attack: the sudden sleepy feeling that one experiences after stuffing him or herself with food

kanaka maoli: Native Hawaiian people

kanikapila: an impromptu Hawaiian music jam session

kau inoa: literally "to place your name" in Hawaiian. Also the name of a Hawaiian rights movement

keiki: Hawaiian word for "child"

koa: a tree endemic to Hawaii

kolohe: Hawaiian word for "rascal"

kui: literally "needle" in Hawaiian. In skin diving, a stinger used to hold speared fish

kuli kuli: "be quiet" or "keep still" in Hawaiian

laulau: a Hawaiian dish that consists of pork wrapped in taro leaf

manini: a small, striped tang (a type of fish)

moke: a slang term that refers to rural Hawaiian males who are uneducated and aggressive (like "redneck" in the South)

Nainoa Thompson: Native Hawaiian navigator and executive director of the Polynesian Voyaging Society

naupaka: a beach shrub indigenous to Hawaii

okolehao: an alcoholic spirit distilled from the ti plant

ono: wahoo (a type of fish)

opakapaka: crimson snapper (a type of fish)

opihi: a type of ocean limpet found in tidal areas

pake: a Chinese person. Also means "cheap" or "stingy" (a racial stereotype)

pau: Hawaiian word for "done" or "finished"

pau hana: Hawaiian phrase for "after work"

shaka: hand gesture in Hawaii that means "hang loose"

The Beamers: Native Hawaiian musician brothers who revolutionized contemporary Hawaiian music

tita: a tough female who is willing to fight

uhu: parrotfish

ulua: a giant trevally (a type of fish)

upepe: flat-nosed

wana: a long-spined venomous sea urchin

An Interview with Chris McKinney

1) *What's the difference between writing fiction versus nonfiction?*

Oddly, the difference was not as great as I'd expected. There were certainly times when I wished I could simply make something up. I also had to make sure that I preserved Rudy's voice, which was challenging at times. Basically, I had to say things the way Rudy would say them, and not the way I would. I also had to resist interjecting my own impressions and opinions. But ultimately, a story is a story, and Rudy and I were just trying to tell a good one.

2) *What would you have done if you had decided to fictionalize Rudy's story?*

I would not have fictionalized it. The story accomplishes what we set out to do as non-fiction. It works better as non-fiction because the whole point of this book is to say this really happened and it can happen for you (the young reader), too. However, I can, say, see myself taking components of particular characters and implementing them in future fictional characters (for example, Rudy's father).

3) *What would you generalize from Rudy's story for Hawaiian youth?*

Don't ever let anyone tell you "no can."

4) *What lessons are there for all youth regardless of background?*

I hate to sound like a parent, but I suppose the big lesson here is work hard and anything is possible. I'd also add that success (and by success, I simply mean getting what one wants, long term, whatever it is), means committing to completing menial tasks that one hates doing. Just doing the stuff one likes is easy. Be tougher than that.

5) *Why do you think so many Hawaiian kids have a hard time?*

Hmm, that's a question with a pretty complicated answer that could easily turn book-length. I guess, to start, we're talking about a people who from the year of Western discovery (1778) to 1900, lost about 90% of its population. Add to that the theft of land and decimation of culture. If anything, the fact that Hawaiians still exist says a lot about Hawaiian resiliency. But many of those who survived exist in a state of poverty, and poverty, no matter where it exists, is crammed with glass ceilings. Another factor is that colonization is not just physical, but mental, too. A colonized people start seeing their self-worth not though their own eyes, but through the eyes of their colonizers. A good example of this is Rudy's father, who for years was ashamed to be Hawaiian, which was not uncommon for that generation which experienced extreme prejudice. Presently, there are still those who cannot see beyond what they perceive as their predestined role (worker, tough guy, dealer, etc.). This is another example of the colonization of the mind.

6) *By showing how one person can overcome, are you saying it's up to the individual and socio-economic factors are just background noise?*

I guess I'm saying socio-economic factors, like poverty, make things tremendously hard—hard, but not impossible. If an individual has hope and is willing to work his or her tail off, overcoming can become a reality. If this book can somehow make just one person believe, then the whole thing was worth it.

7) *Would you call The Red-Headed Hawaiian a memoir or a biography written by a friend?*

I'd call it a memoir since we worked hard to keep his first-person voice intact.

8) *What research did you do for this book?*

I harassed Rudy for half-a-year. I also talked at length with his mother. I considered doing far more research on Nebraska and Texas, but then I realized that if I did so, I'd be in danger of describing my Nebraska and my Texas, which is contrary to the point of the book. This is Rudy's story, and his impressions needed to trump mine.

9) *How did you collaborate—did you do all the writing?*

Rudy gave me what was essentially a freewrite of his life story. I shaped it into a story. This meant cutting stuff, interviewing him, then adding stuff to give the story arc. I just needed to ask the right questions, which was easy because I know him well. Some of his original writing is preserved in the final draft—for example, all the stuff that depicts Rudy fishing with his father is in his words. I could not have written that part any better.

10) *What disagreements, if any, did you have?*

Absolutely none. There was more laughing than anything else during the process. Rudy has always been one of my funniest friends.

11) *What was left out of Rudy's story?*

Just about everything that did not contribute to character arc. Entertaining anecdotes, for example, that would be told just for the sake of entertainment. I tried my best to omit episodes that did not advance story. We also wanted to keep this story PG-13, so younger readers could have access to it.

12) *If Rudy had been a girl, how would the story play out?*

This would have been an easy adjustment. I would have simply written a book about his sister Kathy, whose accomplishments are equally impressive.

13) *How would Rudy's story have been different if he was Black or Hispanic living in a community on the Mainland?*

Though there certainly might have been parallels, one has to remember that being displaced from Hawaii is different than being displaced from, say, the Bayou. Thousands of miles of ocean means there are no road trips back home. Unless you have a lot of time and money, it's difficult to make it back once you're gone.

14) *Did Rudy's family have a chance to read or comment?*

His wife, Lynn, did. No one else as far as I know. I talked to his mother about it (she was a great source of info.). But I think they're all waiting for the printed version to come out.

15) *You write mainly about blue collar, forgotten Hawai'i (except for* **Mililani Mauka***). Kaui Hemmings writes about Outrigger* *and private club privileged people. What would local middle class stories be about?*

My impression of the local middle class is that it is more Americanized than working class and upper class Hawaii. The local culture feels more dead in Hawaii subdivisions than anywhere else in the Islands.

16) *What has kept you from writing a story where a local woman, born in Hawai'i, is the central character?*

A woman from Korea is the central character in my second novel, *The Queen of Tears*. I also wrote a screenplay for producer/director Wayne Wang (*Joy Luck Club, Maid in Manhattan*) that has a female lead (unfortunately, this film did not get made). I'm not saying I'm super good at it, but I've tried it. And I'll probably try it again in the future.

17) *Any advice for young local writers?*

If you decide to write about Hawaii, don't do it just because it's what you know. Do it because you either really love this place or really hate this place, or both. There has to be passion behind the story no matter where it's set. If you do not feel this passion for this place, write about somewhere else.

18) *You have stayed in Hawai'i. Has that insulated your scope?*

Fancy question. I don't think so. There may have been a time when I was tempted to move and write about someplace else, but then I realized most of the writers that I admire most are regional writers. Greats like Faulkner and O'Connor. Present-day talents like Richard Price, Daniel Woodrell, and Richard Russo—they write about the same region for the most part. I doubt any of these writers would be accused of having an insulated scope.

19) *How would your writing career have been different if you had left Hawai'i?*

My guess is I would have become a screenwriter in L.A. chasing dollars. I also believe, like Rudy, I would eventually have come home.

20) *Everyone knows* The Tattoo—*why does that book stand out?*

Readability, relatability—I was twenty-four when I wrote it, and I think that comes off for many young, local readers. It's like listening to one of their peers talk story. But the biggest reason? Ken (the main character) is easy to root for. That's all most readers want. Someone to cheer on. In, say, *Boi No Good*, a more complex (and superior) book, the main character is more difficult to root for, his cause more extreme and unfamiliar. Essentially, *The Tattoo* is filled with enough standard story devices that makes it easy reading—inner conflict, a character who gets what he wants but not in the way he wanted to get it—but it also is a true representation of the values and lifestyle that many of us who grew up in Hawaii are familiar with. It revealed a side of the Hawaii ethos that had not really been written about at length before.

21) *What advice would you give to someone wanting to tell their life story?*

Before writing your life story, read a bunch of other life stories first. Before you start writing, figure out what your life story is about. What has driven you throughout your life? Did you go through changes? Were there profound moments of realization during your lifetime? Did your desires change? If so, why? How does your story end? A memoir is not just a rendering of one's life highlights and lowlights. It's a narrative with rising action, climax, and resolution. In other words, your life story is just that, a story.

About the Authors

Chris McKinney is the author of five novels, *The Tattoo, The Queen of Tears, Bolohead Row, Mililani Mauka,* and *Boi No Good.* He has also written a feature film screenplay, *Paradise Broken* (nominated for best film at the Los Angeles Pacific Film Festival), and a short film, *The Back Door,* both of which premiered at the 2011 Hawai'i International Film Festival.

In 2011, he was appointed Visiting Distinguished Writer at the University of Hawai'i at Mānoa. Over the years, he has won one Elliot Cades Award for Literature from the Hawai'i Literary Arts Council and six Ka Palapala Po'okela Awards (three honorable mentions) from the Hawai'i Book Publishers Association.

Rudolph Puana M.D. is a double-boarded critical care physician. After graduating the University of Hawai'i at Mānoa, he attended Creighton University medical school and received the prestigious Dean's Scholarship—one of the few full-ride scholarships to medical school in the nation.

After completing his residency at Texas A&M University, he accepted a position as a fellow of critical care medicine at the world renowned MD Anderson Cancer Hospital where he became one of the youngest Associate Medical Directors in the hospital's history.

In 2008, he gave up his research lab, patient care, and title and moved to the Big Island of Hawai'i to help the underserved medical community at large. Currently, Dr. Puana is in private practice running his own interventional pain clinic in Hilo, Hawai'i.

To Order Chris McKinney's Books

Visit www.mutualpublishing.com,
email info@mutualpublishing.com
or call 808-732-1709

The Tattoo
4.75 x 7 in.
240 pages, $7.95

The Queen of Tears
4.75 x 7 in.
336 pages, $7.95

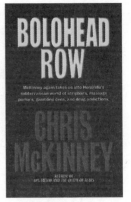

Bolohead Row
5 x 8 in.
224 pages, $13.95

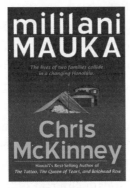

Miliani Mauka
5.5 x 8 in.
240 pages, $12.95

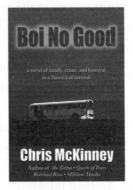

Boi No Good
5.5 x 8 in.
336 pages, $15.95